Suddenly the night was filled with fire rockets that screamed out of the Ark, pillars of flame that stunned the darkness, outreaches of fire searing the heavens. A white circle of light made a flashing ring around the island, a light that made the ocean glow and whipped up currents of spray, forcing a broken tide to rise upward in the dark.

The light, it was the light of the first day of the universe, the light of newness, of things freshly born, it was the light that God made: the light of creation.

RAIDERS OF THE LOST ARK

Novel by Campbell Black

Adapted from a screenplay by
Lawrence Kasdan
Based on a story by
George Lucas and
Philip Kaufman

BALLANTINE BOOKS • NEW YORK

 Published in the United States by Ballantine Books, a division of Random House, Inc., New York, and simultaneously in Canada by Random House of Canada, Limited, Toronto, Canada.

Library of Congress Catalog Card Number: 80-69250

ISBN 0-345-29490-4

Printed in Canada

First Edition: April 1981

RAIDERS OF THE LOST ARK

1: South America, 1936

The jungle was darkly verdant, secretive, menacing. What little sunlight broke the high barriers of branches and twisted vines was pale, milky in color. The air, sticky and solid, created a wall of humidity. Birds screamed in panic, as if they had been unexpectedly trapped in some huge net. Glittering insects scurried underfoot, animals chattered and squealed in the foliage. In its primitive quality the place might have been a lost terrain, a point unmapped, untraveled—the end of the world.

Eight men made their way slowly along a narrow trail, pausing now and then to hack at an overhanging vine or slice at a dangling branch. At the head of this group there was a tall man in a leather jacket and a brimmed felt hat. Behind him were two Peruvians, who regarded the jungle cautiously, and five nervous Quechua Indians, struggling with the pair of donkeys that carried the packs and provisions.

The man who led the group was called Indiana Jones. He was muscular in the way one might associate with an athlete not quite beyond his prime. He had several days' growth of dirty blond beard and streaks of dark sweat on a face that might once have been handsome in a facile, photogenic fashion. Now, though, there were tiny lines around the eyes, the corners of the mouth, changing the almost bland good looks into an expression of character, depth. It was as if the contours of his experience had begun, slowly, to define his appearance.

Indy Jones didn't move with the same caution as the two Peruvians—his confidence made it seem as if he, rather than they, were the native there. But his outward swagger did not impair his sense of alertness. He knew enough to look occasionally, almost imperceptibly, from side to side, to expect the jungle to reveal a threat, a danger, at any moment. The sudden parting of a branch or the cracking of rotted wood—these were the signals, the points on his compass of danger. At times he would pause, take off his hat, wipe sweat from his forehead and wonder what bothered him more—the humidity or the nervousness of the Quechuas. Every so often they would talk excitedly with one another in quick bursts of their strange language, a language that reminded Indy of the sounds of jungle birds, creatures of the impenetrable foliage, the recurring mists.

He looked around at the two Peruvians, Barranca and Satipo, and he realized how little he really trusted them and yet how much he was obliged to depend on them to get what he wanted out of this jungle.

What a crew, he thought. Two furtive Peruvians, five terrified Indians, and two recalcitrant donkeys. And I am their leader, who might have done better with a troop of Boy Scouts.

Indy turned to Barranca and, though he was sure he knew the answer, asked, "What are the Indians talking about?"

Barranca seemed irritated. "What do they always talk about, Señor Jones? The curse. Always the curse."

Indy shrugged and stared back at the Indians. Indy understood their superstitions, their beliefs, and in a way he even sympathized with them. The curse—the ancient curse of the Temple of the Chachapoyan Warriors. The Quechuas had been raised with it; it was intrinsic to their system of beliefs.

He said, "Tell them to be quiet, Barranca. Tell

them no harm will come to them." The salve of words. He felt like a quack doctor administering a dose of an untested serum. How the devil could he know that no harm would come to them?

Barranca watched Indy a moment, then he spoke harshly to the Indians, and for a time they were silent —a silence that was one of repressed fear. Again, Indy felt sympathy for them: vague words of comfort couldn't dispose of centuries of superstition. He put his hat back on and moved slowly along the trail, assailed by the odors of the jungle, the scents of things growing and other things rotting, ancient carcasses crawling with maggots, decaying wood, dying vegetation. You could think of better places to be than here, he thought, you could think of sweeter places.

And then he was wondering about Forrestal, imagining him coming along this same path years ago, imagining the fever in Forrestal's blood when he came close to the Temple. But Forrestal, good as he had been as an archaeologist, hadn't come back from his trip to this place—and whatever secrets that lay contained in the Temple were locked there still. Poor Forrestal. To die in this godforsaken place was a hell of an epitaph. It wasn't one Indy relished for himself.

He moved along the trail again, followed by the group. The jungle lay in a canyon at this point, and the trail traversed the canyon wall like an old scar. There were thin mists rising from the ground now, vapors he knew would become thicker, more dense, as the day progressed. The mists would be trapped in this canyon almost as if they were webs spun by the trees themselves.

A huge macaw, gaudy as a fresh rainbow, screamed out of the underbrush and winged into the trees, momentarily startling him. And then the Indians were jabbering again, gesticulating wildly with their hands, prodding one another. Barranca turned and silenced them with a fierce command—but Indy knew it was going to be more and more difficult to keep them under any kind of control. He could feel their anxieties as certainly as he could the humidity pressing against his flesh.

Besides, the Indians mattered less to him than his growing mistrust of the two Peruvians. Especially Barranca. It was a gut instinct, the kind he always relied on, an intuition he'd felt for most of the journey. But it was stronger now. They'd cut his throat for a few salted peanuts, he knew.

It isn't much farther, he told himself.

And when he realized how close he was to the Temple, when he understood how near he was to the Idol of the Chachapoyans, he experienced the old adrenaline rushing through him: the fulfillment of a dream, an old oath he'd taken for himself, a pledge he'd made when he'd been a novice in archaeology. It was like going back fifteen years into his past, back to the familiar sense of wonder, the obsessive urge to understand the dark places of history, that had first excited him about archaeology. A dream, he thought. A dream taking shape, changing from something nebulous to something tangible. And now he could feel the nearness of the Temple, feel it in the hollows of his bones.

He paused and listened to the Indians chatter again. They too know. *They know how close we are now.* And it scares them. He moved forward. Through the trees there was a break in the canyon wall. The trail was almost invisible: it had been choked by creepers, stifled by bulbous weeds that crawled over roots—roots that had the appearance of growths produced by some floating spores randomly drifting in space, planting themselves here by mere whim. Indy hacked, swinging his arm so that his broad-bladed knife cracked through the obstructions as if they were nothing more than fibrous papers. Damn jungle. You couldn't let nature, even at its most perverse, its most unruly, defeat you. When he paused he was soaked in sweat and his muscles ached. But he felt good as he looked at the slashed creepers, the severed roots. And then he was aware of the mist thickening, not a cold mist, not a chill, but something created out of the sweat of the jungle itself. He caught his breath and moved through the passage.

He caught it again when he reached the end of the trail.

It was there.

There, in the distance, shrouded by thick trees, *the Temple.*

For a second he was seized by the strange linkages of history, a sense of permanence, a continuum that made it possible for someone called Indiana Jones to be alive in the year 1936 and see a construction that had been erected two thousand years before. Awed. Overwhelmed. A humbling feeling. But none of these descriptions was really accurate. There wasn't a word for this excitement.

For a time he couldn't say anything.

He just stared at the edifice and wondered at the energy that had gone into building such a structure in the heart of a merciless jungle. And then he was shaken back into an awareness of the present by the shouts of the Indians, and he swung round to see three of them running back along the trail, leaving the donkeys. Barranca had his pistol out and was leveling it to fire at the fleeing Indians, but Indy gripped the man's wrist, twisted it slightly, swung the Peruvian around to face him.

"No," he said.

Barranca stared at Indy accusingly. "They are cowards, Señor Jones."

"We don't need them," Indy said. "And we don't need to kill them."

The Peruvian brought the pistol to his side, glanced at his companion Satipo and looked back at Indy again. "Without the Indians, Señor, who will carry the supplies? It was not part of our arrangement that Satipo and I do menial labor, no?"

Indy watched the Peruvian, the dark coldness at the heart of the man's eyes. He couldn't ever imagine this one smiling. He couldn't imagine daylight finding its way into Barranca's soul. Indy remembered seeing such dead eyes before: on a shark. "We'll dump the supplies. As soon as we get what we came here for, we can make it back to the plane by dusk. We don't need supplies now."

Barranca was fidgeting with his pistol.

A trigger-happy fellow, Indy thought. Three dead Indians wouldn't make a bit of difference to him.

"Put the gun away," Indy told him. "Pistols don't agree with me, Barranca, unless I'm the one with my finger on the trigger."

Barranca shrugged and glanced at Satipo; some kind of silent communication passed between them. They'll choose their moment, Indy knew. They'll make their move at the right time.

"Just tuck it in your belt, okay?" Indy asked. He looked briefly at the two remaining Indians, herded into place by Satipo. They had trancelike expressions of fear on their faces; they might have been zombies.

Indy turned toward the Temple, gazing at it, savoring the moment. The mists were becoming denser around the place, a conspiracy of nature, as if the jungle intended to keep its secrets forever.

Satipo bent and pulled something out of the bark of a tree. He raised his hand to Indy. In the center of the palm lay a tiny dart.

"Hovitos," Satipo said. "The poison is still fresh—three days, Señor Jones. They must be following us."

"If they knew we were here, they'd have killed us already," Indy said calmly.

He took the dart. Crude but effective. He thought of the Hovitos, their legendary fierceness, their historic attachment to the Temple. They were superstitious enough to stay away from the Temple itself, but definitely jealous enough to kill anybody else who went there.

"Let's go," he said. "Let's get it over with."

They had to hack and slash again, cut and slice through the elaborately tangled vines, rip at the creepers that rose from underfoot like shackles lying in wait. Sweating, Indy paused; he let his knife dangle at his side. From the corner of his eye he was conscious of one of the Indians hauling back a thick branch.

It was the scream that made him swing abruptly round, his knife raised in the air now. It was the wild scream of the Indian that made him rush toward the branch just as the Quechua, still yelling, dashed off into the jungle. The other remaining Indian followed, crashing mindlessly, panicked, against the barbed branches and sharp creepers. And then they were both gone. Indy, knife poised, hauled back the branch that had so scared the Indians. He was ready to lunge at whatever had terrified them, ready to thrust his blade forward. He drew the branch aside.

It sat behind the swirling mist.

Carved out of stone, timeless, its face the figment of some bleak nightmare, it was a sculpture of a Chachapoyan demon. He watched it for a second, aware of the malevolence in its unchanging face, and he realized it had been placed here to guard the Temple, to scare off anybody who might pass this way. A work of art, he thought, and he wondered briefly about its creators, their system of beliefs, about the kind of religious awe that might inspire something so dreadful as this statue. He forced himself to put out his hand and touch the demon lightly on the shoulder.

Then he was conscious of something else, something that was more disturbing than the stone face. More eerie.

The silence.

The weird silence.

Nothing. No birds. No insects. No breeze to shake sounds out of the trees. A zero, as if everything in this place were dead. As if everything had been stilled, silenced by an ungodly, destructive hand. He touched his forehead. Cold, cold sweat. Spooks, he thought. The place is filled with spooks. This was the kind of silence you might have imagined before creation.

He moved away from the stone figure, followed by the two Peruvians, who seemed remarkably subdued.

"What is it, in the name of God?" Barranca asked.

Indy shrugged. "Ah, some old trinket. What else? Every Chachapoyan household had to have one, didn't you know?"

Barranca looked grim. "Sometimes you seem to take this very lightly, Señor Jones."

"Is there another way?"

The mist crawled, rolled, clawed, seeming to press the three men back. Indy peered through the vapors, staring at the Temple entrance, the elaborately primitive friezes that had yielded to vegetation with the passage of time, the clutter of shrubs, leaves, wines; but what held him more was the dark entrance itself, round and open, like the mouth of a corpse. He thought of Forrestal passing into that dark mouth, crossing the entranceway to his death. Poor guy.

Barranca stared at the entranceway. "How can we trust you, Señor Jones? No one has ever come out alive. Why should we put our faith in you?"

Indy smiled at the Peruvian. "Barranca, Barranca—you've got to learn that even a miserable gringo sometimes tells the truth, huh?" And he pulled a piece of folded parchment out of his shirt pocket. He stared at the faces of the Peruvians. Their expressions were transparent, such looks of greed. Indy wondered whose throats had been cut so that these two villains had managed to obtain the other half. "This, Barranca, should take care of your faith," and he spread the parchment on the ground.

Satipo took a similar piece of parchment from his pocket and laid it alongside the one Indy had produced. The two parts dovetailed neatly. For a time, nobody spoke; the threshold of caution had been reached, Indy knew—and he waited, tensely, for something to happen.

"Well, amigos," he said. "We're partners. We have what you might call mutual needs. Between us we have a complete map of the floor plan of the Temple. We've got what nobody else ever had. Now, assuming that pillar there marks the corner—"

Before he could finish his sentence he saw, as if in a slowed reel of film, Barranca reach for his pistol. He saw the thin brown hand curl itself over the butt of the silver gun—and then he moved. Indiana Jones moved faster than the Peruvian could have followed; his motions a blur, a parody of vision, he moved back from Barranca and, reaching under the back of his leather jacket, produced a coiled bullwhip, his hand tight on the handle. His movements became liquid, one fluid and graceful display of muscle and poise and balance, arm and bullwhip seeming to be one thing, extensions of each other. He swung the whip, lashing the air, watching it twist itself tightly around Barranca's wrist. Then he jerked downward, tighter still, and the gun discharged itself into the ground. For a moment the Peruvian didn't move. He stared at Indy in amazement, a mixture of confusion and pain and hatred, loathing the fact that he'd been outsmarted, humiliated. And then, as the whip around his wrist slackened, Barranca turned and ran, racing after the Indians into the jungle.

Indy turned to Satipo. The man raised his hands in the air.

"Señor, please," he said, "I knew nothing, nothing of his plan. He was crazy. A crazy man. Please, Señor. Believe me."

Indy watched him a moment, then nodded and picked up the pieces of the map.

"You can drop your hands, Satipo."

The Peruvian looked relieved and lowered his arms stiffly.

"We've got the floor plan," Indy said. "So what are we waiting for?"

And he turned toward the Temple entrance.

The smell was the scent of centuries, the trapped odors of years of silence and darkness, of the damp flowing in from the jungle, the festering of plants. Water dripped from the ceiling, slithered through the mosses that had grown there. The passageway whispered with the scampering of rodent claws. And the air—the air was unexpectedly cold, untouched by sunlight, forever shaded. Indy walked ahead of Satipo, listening to the echoes of their footsteps. Alien sounds, he thought. A disturbance of the dead—and for a moment he was touched by the feeling of being in the wrong place at the wrong time, like a plunderer, a looter, someone intent on damaging things that have lain too long in peace.

He knew the feeling well, a sense of wrongdoing. It wasn't the sort of emotion he enjoyed entertaining because it was like having a boring guest at an otherwise decent dinner party He watched his shadow move in the light of the torch Satipo carried.

The passageway twisted and turned as it bored deeper into the interior of the Temple. Every now and then Indy would stop and look at the map, by the light of the torch, trying to remember the details of the layout. He wanted to drink, his throat was dry, his tongue parched—but he didn't want to stop. He could hear a clock tick inside his skull, and every tick was telling him, *You don't have time, you don't have time*. . .

The two men passed ledges carved out of the walls. Here and there Indy would stop and examine the artifacts that were located on the ledges. He would sift through them, discarding some expertly, placing others in his pockets. Small coins, tiny medallions, pieces of pottery small enough to carry on his person. He knew what was valuable and what wasn't. But they were nothing in comparison to what he'd really come for—the Idol.

He moved more quickly now, the Peruvian rushing behind him, panting as he hurried to keep up. And then Indy stopped suddenly, joltingly.

"Why have we stopped?" Satipo asked, his voice sounding as if his lungs were on fire.

Indy said nothing, remained frozen, barely breathing. Satipo, confused, took one step toward Indy, went to touch him on the arm, but he too stopped and let his hand freeze in midair.

A huge black tarantula crawled up Indy's back, maddeningly slowly. Indy could feel its legs as they inched toward the bare skin of his neck. He waited, waited for what seemed like forever, until he felt the horrible creature settle on his shoulder. He could feel Satipo's panic, could sense the man's desire to scream and jump. He knew he had to move quickly, yet casually so Satipo would not run. Indy, in one smooth motion, flicked his hand over his shoulder and knocked the creature away into the shadows. Relieved, he began to move forward but then he heard Satipo's gasp, and turned to see two more spiders drop onto the Peruvian's arm. Instinctively, Indy's whip lashed out from the shadows, throwing the creatures onto the ground. Quickly, Indy stepped on the scuttling spiders, stomping them beneath his boot.

Satipo paled, seemed about to faint. Indy grabbed him, held him by the arm until he was steady. And then the archaelogist pointed down the hallway at a small chamber ahead, a chamber which was lit by a single shaft of sunlight from a hole in the ceiling. The tarantulas were forgotten; Indy knew other dangers lay ahead.

"Enough, Señor," Satipo breathed. "Let us go back."

But Indy said nothing. He continued to gaze toward the chamber, his mind already working, figuring, his imagination helping him to think his way inside the minds of the people who had built this place so long ago. They would want to protect the treasure of the Temple, he thought. They would want to erect barricades, traps, to make sure no stranger ever reached the heart of the Temple.

He moved closer to the entrance now, moving with the instinctive caution of the hunter who smells danger on the downwind, who feels peril before he can see signs of it. He bent down, felt around on the floor, found a thick stalk of a weed, hauled it out—then reached forward and tossed the stalk into the chamber.

For a split second nothing happened. And then there was a faint whirring noise, a creaking sound, and the walls of the chamber seemed to break open as giant metal spikes, like the jaws of some impossible shark, slammed together in the center of the chamber. Indiana Jones smiled, appreciating the labors of the Temple designers, the cunning of this horrible trap. The Peruvian swore under his breath, crossed himself. Indy was about to say something when he noticed an object impaled on the great spikes. It took only a moment for him to realize the nature of the thing that had been sliced through by the sharp metal.

"Forrestal."

Half skeleton. Half flesh. The face grotesquely preserved by the temperature of the chamber, the pained surprise still apparent, as if it had been left unchanged as a warning to anybody else who might want to enter the room. Forrestal, impaled through chest and groin, blackened blood visible on his jungle khakis, death stains. Jesus, Indy thought. Nobody deserved to go like this. Nobody. He experienced a second of sadness. You just blundered into it, pal. You were out of your league. You should have stayed in the classroom. Indy shut his eyes briefly, then stepped inside the chamber and dragged the remains of the man from the tips of the spikes, laying the corpse on the floor.

"You knew this person?" Satipo asked.

"Yeah, I knew him."

The Peruvian made the sign of the cross again. "I think, Señor, we should perhaps go no further."

"You wouldn't let a little thing like this discourage you, would you, Satipo?" Then Indy didn't speak for a time. He watched the metal spikes begin to retract slowly, sliding back toward the walls from which they'd emerged. He marveled at the simple mechanics of the arrangement—simple and deadly.

Indy smiled at the Peruvian, momentarily touching him on the shoulder. The man was sweating profusely, trembling. Indy stepped inside the chamber, wary of the spikes, seeing their ugly tips set into the walls. After a time the Peruvian, grunting, whispering to himself, followed. They passed through the chamber and emerged into a straight hallway some fifty feet long. At the end of the passageway there was a door, bright with sunlight streaming from above.

"We're close," Indy said, "so close."

He studied the map again before folding it, the details memorized. But he didn't move immediately. His eyes scanned the place for more traps, more pitfalls.

"It looks safe," Satipo said.

"That's what scares me, friend."

"It's safe," the Peruvian said again. "Let's go."

Satipo, suddenly eager, stepped forward.

And then he stopped as his right foot slipped through the surface of the floor. He flew forward, screaming. Indy moved quickly, grabbed the Peruvian by his belt and hauled him up to safety. Satipo fell to the ground exhausted.

Indy looked down at the floor through which the Peruvian had stepped. Cobwebs, an elaborate expanse of ancient cobwebs, over which lay a film of dust, creating the illusion of a floor. He bent down, picked up a stone and dropped it through the surface of webs. Nothing, no sound, no echo came back.

"A long way down," Indy muttered.

Satipo, breathless, said nothing.

Indy stared across the surface of webs toward the sunlit door. How to cross the space, the pit, when the floor doesn't exist?

Staipo said, "I think now we go back, Señor. No?"

"No," Indy said. "I think we go forward."

"How? With wings? Is that what you think?"

"You don't need wings in order to fly, friend."

He took out his whip and stared up at the ceiling. There were various beams set into the roof. They might be rotted through, he thought. On the other hand, they might be strong enough to hold his weight. It was worth a try, anyhow. If it didn't work, he'd have to kiss the idol good-bye. He swung the whip upward, seeing it coil around a beam, then he tugged on the whip and tested it for strength.

Satipo shook his head. "No. You're crazy."

"Can you think of a better way, friend?"

"The whip will not hold us. The beam will snap."

"Save me from pessimists," Indy said. "Save me from disbelievers. Just trust me. Just do what I do, okay?"

Indy curled both hands around the whip, pulled on it again to test it, then swung himself slowly through the air, conscious all the time of the illusory floor underneath him, of the darkness of the pit that lay deep below the layers of cobwebs and dust, aware of the possibility that the beam might snap, the whip work itself loose, and then . . . but he didn't have time to consider these bleak things. He swung, clutching the whip, feeling air rush against him. He swung until he was sure he was beyond the margins of the pit and then he lowered himself, coming down on solid ground. He pushed the whip back across to the Peruvian, who muttered something in Spanish under his breath, something Indy was sure had religious significance. He wondered idly if there might exist, somewhere in the vaults of the Vatican, a patron saint for those who had occasion to travel by whip.

He watched the Peruvian land beside him.

"Told you, didn't I? Beats traveling by bus."

Satipo said nothing. Even in the dim light, Indy could see his face was pale. Indy now wedged the handle of the bullwhip against the wall. "For the return trip," he said. "I never go anywhere one way, Satipo."

The Peruvian shrugged as they moved through the sunlit doorway into a large domed room, the ceiling of which had skylights that sent bands of sunlight down on the black-and-white tiled floor. And then Indy noticed something on the other side of the chamber, something that took his breath away, filled him with awe, with a pleasure he could barely define.

The Idol.

Set on some kind of altar, looking both fierce and lovely, its gold shape glittering in the flames of the torch, shining in the sunlight that slipped through the roof—*the Idol.*

The Idol of the Chachapoyan Warriors.

What he felt then was the excitement of an overpowering lust, the desire to race across the room and touch its beauty—a beauty surrounded by obstacles and traps. And what kind of booby trap was saved for last? What kind of trap surrounded the Idol itself?

"I'm going in," he said.

The Peruvian now also saw the Idol and said nothing. He stared at the figurine with an expression of avarice that suggested he was suddenly so possessed by greed that nothing else mattered except getting his hands on it. Indy watched him a moment, thinking, *He's seen it. He's seen its beauty. He can't be trusted.* Satipo was about to step beyond the threshold when Indy stopped him.

"Remember Forrestal?" Indy said.

"I remember."

He stared across the intricate pattern of black-and-white tiles, wondering about the precision of the arrangement, about the design. Beside the doorway there were two ancient torches in rusted metal holders. He reached up, removed one, trying to imagine the face of the last person who might have held this very torch; the span of time—it never failed to amaze him that the least important of objects endured through centuries. He lit it, glanced at Satipo, then bent down and pressed the unlit end against one of the white tiles. He tapped it. Solid. No echo, no resonance. Very solid. He next tapped one of the black tiles.

It happened before he could move his hand away. A noise, the sound of something slamming through the air, something whistling with the speed of its movement, and a small dart drove itself into the shaft of his torch. He pulled his hand away. Satipo exhaled quietly, then pointed inside the room.

"It came from there," he said. "You see that hole? The dart came from there."

"I also see hundreds of other holes," Indy said. The place, the whole place, was honeycombed with shadowy recesses, each of which would contain a dart, each of which would release its missile whenever there was pressure on a black tile.

"Stay here, Satipo."

Slowly, the Peruvian turned his face. "If you insist."

Indy, holding the lit torch, moved cautiously into the chamber, avoiding the black tiles, stepping over them to reach the safe white ones. He was conscious of his shadow thrown against the walls of the room by the light of the torch, conscious of the wicked holes, seen now in half-light, that held the darts. Mainly, though, it was the idol that demanded his attention, the sheer beauty of it that became more apparent the closer he got to it, the hypnotic glitter, the enigmatic expression on the face. Strange, he thought: six inches high, two thousand years old, a lump of gold whose face could hardly be called lovely—strange that men would lose their minds for this, kill for this. And yet it mesmerized him and he had to look away. Concentrate on the tiles, he told himself. Only the tiles. Nothing else. Don't lose the fine edge of your instinct here.

Underfoot, sprawled on a white tile and riddled with darts, lay a small dead bird. He stared at it, sickened for a moment, seized by the realization that whoever had built this Temple, whoever had planned the traps, would have been too cunning to booby trap only the black tiles: like a wild card in a deck, at least one white tile would have been poisoned.

At least one.

What if there were others?

He hesitated, sweating now, feeling the sunlight from above, feeling the heat of the torch flame on his face. Carefully, he stepped around the dead bird and looked at the white tiles that lay between himself and the Idol as if each were a possible enemy. Sometimes, he thought, caution alone doesn't carry the day. Sometimes you don't get the prize by being hesitant, by failing to take the final risk. Caution has to be married with chance—but then, you need to know in some way the odds are on your side. The sight of the Idol drew him again. It magnetized him. And he was aware of Satipo behind him, watching from the doorway, no doubt planning his own treachery.

Do it, he said to himself. What the hell. Do it and caution be damned.

He moved with the grace of a dancer. He moved with the strange elegance of a man weaving between razor blades. Every tile now was a possible land mine, a depth charge.

He edged forward and stepped over the black

squares, waiting for the pressure of his weight to trigger the mechanism that would make the air scream with darts. And then he was closer to the altarpiece, closer to the idol. The prize. The triumph. And the last trap of all.

He paused again. His heart ran wildly, his pulses thudded, the blood burned in his veins. Sweat fell from his forehead and slicked across his eyelids, blinding him. He wiped at it with the back of his hand. A few more feet, he thought. A few more feet.

And a few more tiles.

He moved again, raising his legs and then gently lowering them. If he ever needed balance, it was now. The idol seemed to wink at him, to entice him.

Another step.

Another step.

He put his right leg forward, touching the last white tile before the altar.

He'd made it. He'd done it. He pulled a liquor flask from his pocket, uncapped it, drank hard from it. This one you deserve, he thought. Then he stuck the flask away and stared at the idol. The last trap, he wondered. What could the last trap be? The final hazard of all.

He thought for a long time, tried to imagine himself into the minds of the people who'd created this place, who'd constructed these defenses. Okay, somebody comes to take the idol away, which means it has to be lifted, it has to be removed from the slab of polished stone, it has to be *physically* taken.

Then what?

Some kind of mechanism under the idol detects the absence of the thing's weight, and that triggers—what? More darts? No, it would be something even more destructive than that. Something more deadly. He thought again; his mind sped, his nerves pulsated. He bent down and stared around the base of the altar. There were chips of stone, dirt, grit, the accumulation of centuries. Maybe, he thought. Just maybe. He took a small drawstring bag from his pocket, opened it, emptied out the coins it contained, then began to fill the bag with dirt and stones. He weighed it in the palm of his hand for a while. Maybe, he thought again. If you could do it quickly enough. You could do it with the kind of speed that might defeat the mechanism. If that was indeed the kind of trap involved here.

If if if. Too many hypotheticals.

Under other circumstances he knew he would walk away, avoid the consequences of so many intangibles. But not now, not here. He stood upright, weighed the bag again, wondered if it was the same weight as the idol, hoped that it was. Then he moved quickly, picking up the idol and setting the bag down in its place, setting it down on the polished stone.

Nothing. For a long moment, nothing.

He stared at the bag, then at the idol in his hand, and then he was aware of a strange, distant noise, a rumbling like that of a great machine set in motion, a sound of things waking from a long sleep, roaring and tearing and creaking through the spaces of the Temple. The polished stone pedestal suddenly dropped—five inches, six. And then the noise was greater, deafening, and everything began to shake, tremble, as if the very foundations of the place were coming apart, splitting, opening, bricks and wood splintering and cracking.

He turned and moved quickly back across the tiles, moving as fast as he could toward the doorway. And still the noise, like desperate thunder, grew and rolled and echoed through the old hallways and passages and chambers. He moved toward Satipo, who was standing in the doorway with a look of absolute terror on his face.

Now everything was shaking, everything moving, bricks collapsing, walls toppling, everything. When he reached the doorway he turned to see a rock fall across the tiled floor, setting off the darts, which flew pointlessly in their thousands through the disintegrating chamber.

Satipo, breathing hard, had moved toward the whip and was swinging himself across the pit. When he reached the other side he regarded Indy a moment.

I knew it was coming, Indy thought.

I felt it, I knew it, and now that it's about to happen, what can I do? He watched Satipo haul the whip from the beam and gather it in his hand.

"A bargain, Señor. An exchange. The idol for the whip. You throw me the idol, I throw you the whip."

Indy listened to the destruction behind him and watched Satipo.

"What choices do you have, Señor Jones?" Satipo asked.

"Suppose I drop the Idol into the pit, my friend? All you've got for your troubles is a bullwhip, right?"

"And what exactly have *you* got for *your* troubles, Señor?"

Indy shrugged. The noise behind him was growing; he could feel the Temple tremble, the floor begin to sway. The idol, he thought—he couldn't just let the thing fall into the abyss like that.

"Okay, Satipo. The idol for the whip." And he tossed the idol toward the Peruvian. He watched as Satipo seized the relic, stuffed it in his pocket and then dropped the whip on the floor.

Satipo smiled. "I am genuinely sorry, Señor Jones. Adios. And good luck."

"You're no more sorry than me," Indy shouted as he watched the Peruvian disappear down the passageway. The whole structure, like some vengeful deity of the jungle, shook even more.

He heard the sound of more stones falling, pillars toppling. *The curse of the idol,* he thought. It was a matinee movie, it was the kind of thing kids watched wild-eyed on Saturday afternoons in dark cinemas. There was only one thing to do—one thing, no alternative. You have to jump, he realized. You have to take your chances and jump across the pit and hope that gravity is on your side. All hell is breaking loose behind you and there's a godawful abyss just in front of you. So you jump, you wing it into darkness and keep your fingers crossed.

Jump!

He took a deep breath, swung himself out into the air above the pit, swung himself hard as he could, listened to the *swish* of the air around him as he moved. He would have prayed if he were the praying kind, prayed he didn't get swallowed up by the dark nothingness below.

He was dropping now. The impetus was gone from his leap. He was falling. He hoped he was falling on the other side of the pit.

But he wasn't.

He could feel the darkness, dank smelling and damp, rush upward from below, and he threw his hands out, looking for something to grip, some edge, anything to hold on to. He felt his fingertips dig into the edge of the pit, the crumbling edge, and he tried to drag himself upward while the edge yielded and gave way and loose stones dropped into the chasm. He swung his legs, clawed with his hands, struggled like a beached fish to get up, get out, reach whatever might pass now for safety. Straining, groaning, thrashing with his legs against the inside wall of the pit, he struggled to raise himself. He couldn't let the treacherous Peruvian get away with the idol. He swung his legs again, kicked, looked for some kind of leverage that would help him climb up from the pit, something, anything, it didn't matter what. And still the Temple was falling apart like a pathetic straw hut in a hurricane. He grunted, dug his fingers into the ledge above, strained until he thought his muscles might pop, his blood vessels burst, hauled himself up even as he heard the sound of his fingernails breaking with the weight of his body.

Harder, he thought.

Try harder.

He pushed, sweat blinded him, his nerves began to tremble. Something's going to snap, he thought. Something's going to give and then you'll find out exactly what lies at the bottom of this pit. He paused, tried to regroup his strength, rearrange his waning energies, then he hauled himself up again through laborious and wearisome inches.

At last he was able to swing his leg over the top, to slither over the edge to the relative safety of the floor—a floor that was shaking, threatening to split apart at any moment.

He raised himself shakily to a standing position and looked down the hallway in the direction Satipo had taken. He had gone toward the room where Forrestal's remains had been found. The room of spikes. The torture chamber. And suddenly Indy knew what would happen to the Peruvian, suddenly he knew the man's fate even before he heard the terrible clang of the spikes, even before he heard the Peruvian's awful scream echo along the passageway. He listened, reached down for his whip, then ran toward the chamber. Satipo hung to one side, impaled like a grotesquely large butterfly in some madman's collection.

"Adios, Satipo," Indy said, then slipped the idol from the dead man's pocket, edged his way past the spikes and raced into the passageway beyond.

Ahead, he saw the exit, the opening of light, the stand of thick trees beyond. And still the rolling sound increased, filling his ears, vibrating through his body. He turned, astounded to see a vast boulder roll down the passageway toward him, gathering speed as it coursed forward. *The last booby trap,* he thought. They wanted to make sure that even if you got inside the Temple, even if you avoided everything the place could throw at you, then you weren't going to get out alive. He raced. He sprinted insanely toward the exit as the great stone crushed along the passageway behind him. He threw himself forward toward the opening of light and hit the thick grass outside just before the boulder slammed against the exit, sealing the Temple shut forever.

Exhausted, out of breath, he lay on his back.

Too close, he thought. Too close for any form of comfort. He wanted to sleep. He wanted nothing more than the chance to close his eyes, transport himself into the darkness that brings relief, dreamless and deep relief. You could have died a hundred deaths in there, he realized. You could have died more deaths than any man might expect in a lifetime. And then he smiled, sat up, turned the idol around and around in his hands.

But worth it, he thought. Worth the whole thing.

He stared at the golden piece.

He was still staring at it when he saw a shadow fall across him.

The shadow startled him into a sitting position. Squinting, he looked up. There were two Hovitos warriors looking down at him, their faces painted in the ferocious colors of battle, their long bamboo blowguns held erect as spears. But it wasn't the presence of the Indians that worried Indy now; it was the sight of the white man who stood between them in a safari outfit and pith helmet. For a long time Indy said nothing, letting the full sense of recognition dawn on him. The man in the pith helmet smiled, and the smile was frost, lethal.

"Belloq," Indy said.

Of all the people in the world, Belloq.

Indy looked away from the Frenchman's face for a moment, glanced down at the idol in his hand, then stared beyond Belloq to the edge of the trees, where there were about thirty more Hovitos warriors standing in a line. And next to the Indians stood Barranca. Barranca, staring past Indy with a stupid, greedy smile on his face. A smile that turned slowly to a look of bewilderment and then, more rapidly, to a cold, vacant expression, which Indy recognized as signaling death.

The Indians on either side of the traitorous Peruvian released his arms, and Barranca toppled forward. His back was riddled with darts.

"My dear Dr. Jones," Belloq said. "You have a knack of choosing quite the wrong friends."

Indy said nothing. He watched Belloq reach down and pick the idol from his hand. Belloq savored the relic for a time, turning it this way and that, his expression one of deep appreciation.

Belloq nodded his head slightly, a curt gesture that suggested an incongruous politeness, a sense of civility.

"You may have thought I'd given up. But again we see there is nothing you can possess which I cannot take away."

Indy looked in the direction of the warriors. "And the Hovitos expect you to hand the idol over to them?"

"Quite," Belloq said.

Indy laughed. "Naïve of them."

"As you say," Belloq remarked. "If only you spoke their language, you could advise them otherwise, of course."

"Of course," Indy said.

He watched as Belloq turned toward the grouped warriors and lifted the idol in the air; and then, in a remarkable display of unified movement that might have been choreographed, rehearsed, the warriors laid themselves face down on the ground. A moment of sudden stillness, of primitive religious awe. In other circumstances, Indy thought, I might be impressed enough to hang around and watch.

In other circumstances, but not now.

He raised himself slowly to his knees, looked at the back of Belloq, glanced quickly once more at the prostrate warriors—and then he was off, moving fast, running toward the trees, waiting for that moment when the Indians would raise themselves up and the air would be dense with darts from the blowguns.

He plunged into the trees when he heard Belloq shout from behind, screaming in a language that was presumably that of the Hovitos, and then he was sprinting through the foliage, back to the river and the amphibian plane. Run. Run even when you don't have a goddamn scrap of energy left. Find something in reserve.

Just run.

And then he heard the darts.

He heard them shaft the air, whizzing, zinging, creating a melody of death. He ran in a zigzag, moving in a serpentine fashion through the foliage. From behind he could hear the breaking of branches, the crushing of plants, as the Hovitos pursued him. He felt strangely detached all at once from his own body; he'd moved beyond a sense of his physical self, beyond the absurd demands of muscle and sinew, pushing himself through the terrain in a way that was automatic, a matter of basic reflex. He heard the occasional dart strike bark, the scared flapping of jungle birds rising out of branches, the squeal of animals that scampered from the path of the Hovitos. Run, he kept thinking. Run until you can't run anymore, then you run a little further. Don't think. Don't stop.

Belloq, he thought. *My time will come.*

If I get out of this one.

Running—he didn't know for how long. Day was beginning to fade.

He paused, looked upward at the thin light through the dense trees, then dashed in the direction of the river. What he wanted to hear more than anything now was the vital sound of rushing water, what he wanted to see was the waiting plane.

He twisted again and moved through a clearing, where he was suddenly exposed by the absence of trees. For a moment, the clearing was menacing, the sudden silence of dusk unsettling.

Then he heard the cries of the Hovitos, and the clearing seemed to him like the center of a bizarre target. He turned around, saw the movement of a couple of figures, felt the air rush as two spears spun past him—and after that he was running again, racing for the river. He thought as he ran, *They don't teach you survival techniques in Archaeology 101, they don't supply survival manuals along with the methodology of excavation.*

And they certainly don't warn you about the cunning of a Frenchman named Belloq.

He paused again and listened to the Indians behind

him. Then there was another sound, one that delighted him, that exalted him: the motion of fast-flowing water, the swaying of rushes. *The river!* How far could it be now? He listened again to be certain and then moved in the direction of the sound, his energies recharged, batteries revitalized. Quicker now, harder and faster. Crashing through the foliage that slashes against you, ignore the cuts and abrasions. Quicker and harder and faster. The sound was becoming clearer. The water rushing.

He emerged from the trees.

There.

Down the slope, beyond the greenery, the hostile vegetation, the river.

The river and the amphibian plane floating up and down on the swell. He couldn't have imagined anything more welcoming. He moved along the slope and then realized there wasn't an easy way down through the foliage to the plane. There wasn't time to find one, either. You had to go up the slope to the point where, as it formed a cliff over the river, you would have to jump. Jump, he thought. What the hell. What's one more jump?

He climbed, conscious of the shape of a man who sat on one wing of the plane far below. Indy reached a point almost directly over the plane, stared down for a moment, and then he shut his eyes and stepped out over the edge of the cliff.

He hit the tepid water close to the wing of the plane, went under as the current pulled him away, surfaced blindly and struck out toward the craft. The man on the wing stood upright as Indy grabbed a strut and hauled himself out of the water.

"Get the thing going, Jock!" Indy shouted. "Get it going!"

Jock rushed along the wing and clambered inside the cockpit as Indy scurried, breathless, into the passenger compartment and slumped across the seat. He closed his eyes and listened to the shudder of engines when the craft skimmed the surface of the water.

"I didn't expect you to drop in quite so suddenly," Jock said.

"Spare me the puns, huh?"

"A spot of trouble, laddie?"

Indy wanted to laugh. "Remind me to tell you sometime." He lay back and closed his eyes, hoping sleep would come. But then he realized that the plane wasn't moving. He sat upright and leaned forward toward the pilot.

"Stalled," Jock said.

"Stalled! Why?"

Jock grinned. "I only fly the bloody thing. People have this funny impression that all Scotsmen are bloody mechanics, Indy."

Through the window, Indy could see the Hovitos begin to wade into the shallows of the river. Thirty feet, twenty now. They were like grotesque ghosts of the riverbed risen to avenge some historic transgression. They raised their arms; a storm of spears flew toward the fuselage of the plane.

"Jock . . ."

"I'm bloody well trying, Indy. I'm trying."

Calmly, Indy said, "I think you should try harder."

The spears struck the plane, clattering against the wings, hitting the fuselage with the sound of enormous hailstones.

"I've got it," Jock said.

The engines spluttered into laborious life just as two of the Hovitos had swum as far as the wing and were clambering up.

"It's moving," Jock said. "It's moving."

The craft skimmed forward again and then began to rise, with a cumbersome quality, above the river. Indy watched the two warriors lose their balance and drop, like weird creatures of the jungle, into the water.

The plane was rising across the tops of trees, the underdraft shaking the branches, driving panicked birds into the last of sunlight. Indy laughed and closed his eyes.

"Thought you might not make it," Jock said. "To tell you the bloody truth."

"Never a doubt in mind," Indy said, and smiled.

"Relax, now, man. Get some sleep. Forget the bloody jungle."

For a moment, Indy drifted. Relief. The relaxation of muscle. A good feeling. He could lose himself in this sensation for a long time.

Then something moved across his thigh. Something slow, heavy.

He opened his eyes and saw a boa constrictor coiling itself in a threatening way around his upper leg. He jumped upright quickly.

"Jock!"

The pilot looked round, smiled. "He won't hurt you, Indy. That's Reggie. He wouldn't harm a soul."

"Get it away from me, Jock."

The pilot reached back, stroked the snake, then drew it into the cockpit beside him. Indy watched the snake slide away from him. An old revulsion, an inexplicable terror. For some people it was spiders, for some rats, for others enclosed spaces. For him it was the repulsive sight and touch of a snake. He rubbed at the sweat newly formed on his forehead, shivering as the water soaking his clothes turned abruptly chill.

"Just keep it beside you," he said. "I can't stand snakes."

"I'll let you in on a wee secret," Jock said. "The average snake is nicer than the average person."

"I'll take your word for it," Indy said. "Just keep it away from me."

You think you're safe, then—a boa constrictor decides to bask on your body. All in a day's work, he thought.

For a while he looked out of the window and watched darkness fall with an inscrutable certainty over the vast jungle. You can keep your secrets, Indy thought. You can keep all your secrets.

Before he fell asleep, lulled by the noise of the engines, he hoped it would not be a long time before his path crossed once again with that of the Frenchman.

[illegible]

[illegible]

[illegible]

[illegible]

[illegible]

[illegible]

[illegible]

[illegible]

[illegible]

[illegible]

[illegible]

[illegible]

2: Berlin

In an office on the Wilhelmstrasse, an officer in the black uniform of the SS—an incongruously petite man named Eidel—was seated behind his desk, staring at the bundles of manila folders stacked neatly in front of him. It was clear to Eidel's visitor, who was named Dietrich, that the small man used the stacks of folders in a compensatory way: they made him feel big, important. It was the same everywhere these days, Dietrich thought. You assess a man and his worth by the amount of paperwork he is able to amass, by the number of rubber stamps he is authorized to use. Dietrich, who liked to consider himself a man of action, sighed inwardly and looked toward the window, against which a pale brown blind had been drawn. He waited for Eidel to speak, but the SS officer had been silent some time, as if even his silences were intended to convey something of what he saw as his own importance.

Dietrich looked at the portrait of the Führer hanging on the wall. When it came down to it, it didn't matter what you might think of someone like Eidel—soft, shackled to his desk, pompous, locked away in miserable offices—because Eidel had a direct line of access to Hitler. So you listened, and you smiled, and you pretended you were of lesser rank. Eidel, after all, was a member of the inner circle, the elite corps of Hitler's own private guard.

Eidel smoothed his uniform, which looked as if it had been freshly laundered. He said, "I trust I have made the importance of this matter clear to you, Colonel?"

Dietrich nodded. He felt impatient. He hated offices.

Eidel rose, stretched on his tiptoes in the manner of a man reaching for a subway strap he knows to be out of range, then walked to the window. "The Führer has his mind set on obtaining this particular object. And when his mind is set, of course . . ." Eidel paused, turned, stared at Dietrich. He made a gesture with his hands, indicating that whatever passed through the Führer's mind was incomprehensible to lesser men.

"I understand," Dietrich said, drumming his fingertips on his attaché case.

"The religious significance is important," Eidel said. "It isn't that the Führer has any special interest in Jewish relics per se, naturally." And here he paused, laughing oddly, as if the thought were wildly amusing. "He has more interest in the *symbolic* meaning of the item, if you understand."

It crossed Dietrich's mind that Eidel was lying, obscuring something here: it was hard to imagine the Führer's being interested in *anything* for its symbolic value. He stared at the flimsy cable Eidel had allowed him to read a few minutes ago. Then he gazed once more at the picture of Hitler, which was unsmiling, grim.

Eidel, in the manner of a small-town university professor, said, "We come to the matter of expert knowledge now."

"Indeed," Dietrich said.

"We come to the matter, specifically, of archaeological knowledge."

Dietrich said nothing. He saw where this was leading. He saw what was needed of him.

He said, "I'm afraid it's beyond my grasp."

Eidel smiled thinly. "But you have connections, I understand. You have connections with the highest authorities in this field, am I right?"

"A matter of debate."

"There is no time for any such debate," Eidel said. "I am not here to argue the matter of what constitutes high authority, Colonel. I am here, as you are, to obey a certain important order."

"You don't need to remind *me* of that," Dietrich said.

"I know," Eidel said, leaning against his desk now. "And you understand I am talking about a certain authority of your acquaintance whose expertise in this particular sphere of interest will be invaluable to us. Correct?"

"The Frenchman," Dietrich said.

"Of course."

Dietrich was silent for a time. He felt slightly uneasy. It was as if the face of Hitler were scolding him now for his hesitance. "The Frenchman is hard to find. Like any mercenary, he regards the world as his place of employment."

"When did you last hear of him?"

Dietrich shrugged. "In South America, I believe."

Eidel studied the backs of his hands, thin and pale and yet indelicate, like the hands of someone who has failed in his ambition to be a concert pianist. He said, "You can find him. You understand what I'm saying? You understand where this order comes from?"

"I can find him," Dietrich said. "But I warn you now—"

"Don't warn *me*, Colonel."

Dietrich felt his throat become dry. This little trumped-up imbecile of a desk clerk. He would have enjoyed throttling him, stuffing those manila folders down his gullet until he choked. "Very well, I *advise* you—the Frenchman's price is high."

"No object," Eidel said.

"And his trustworthiness is less than admirable."

"That is something you will be expected to deal with. The point, Colonel Dietrich, is that you will find him and you will bring him to the Führer. But it must be done quickly. It must be done, if you understand, *yesterday*."

Dietrich stared at the shade on the window. It sometimes filled him with dread that the Führer had surrounded himself with lackeys and fools like Eidel. It implied a certain cloudiness of judgment where humans were concerned.

Eidel smiled, as if he was amused by Dietrich's unease. Then he said, "Speed is important, of course. Other parties are interested, obviously. These parties do not represent the best interests of the Reich. Do I make myself clear?"

"Clear," Dietrich said. Dietrich thought about the Frenchman for a moment; he knew, even if he hadn't told Eidel, that Belloq was in the south of France right then. The prospect of doing business with Belloq was what appalled him. There was a smooth quality to the man that masked an underlying ruthlessness, a selfishness, a disregard for philosophies, beliefs, politics. If it served Belloq's interests, it was therefore valid. If not, he didn't care.

"The other parties will be taken care of if they should surface," Eidel was saying. "They should be of no concern to you."

"Then that is how I'll treat them," Dietrich said.

Eidel picked up the cable and glanced at it. "What we have talked about is not to go beyond these four walls, Colonel. I don't have to say that, do I?"

"You don't have to say it," Dietrich repeated, irritated.

Eidel went back to his seat and stared at the other man across the mountain of folders. He was silent for a moment. And then he feigned surprise at finding Dietrich seated opposite him. "Are you still here, Colonel?"

Dietrich clutched his attaché case and rose. It was

hard not to feel hatred toward these black-uniformed clowns. They acted as if they owned the world.

"I was about to leave," Dietrich said.

"Heil Hitler," Eidel said, raising his hand, his arm rigid.

At the door Dietrich answered in the same words.

3: Connecticut

Indiana Jones sat in his office at Marshall College.

He had just finished his first lecture of the year for Archaeology 101, and it had gone well. It always went well. He loved teaching and he knew he was able to convey his passion for the subject matter to his students. But now he was restless and his restlessness disturbed him. Because he knew exactly what it was he wanted to do.

Indy put his feet up on the desk, deliberately knocked a couple of books over, then rose and paced around the office—seeing it not as the intimate place it usually was, his retreat, his hideaway, but as the cell of some remote stranger.

Jones, he told himself.

Indiana Jones, wise up.

The objects around him seemed to shed their meaning for a time. The huge wall map of South America became a surreal blur, an artist's dadaist conception. The clay replica of the idol looked suddenly silly, ugly. He picked it up and he thought: For something like *this* you laid your life on the line? You must have an essential screw loose. A bolt out of place.

He held the replica of the idol, gazing at it absently.

This mad love of antiquity struck him all at once as

unholy, unnatural. An insane infatuation with the sense of history—more than the *sense,* the need to reach out and touch it, hold it, understand it through its relics and artifacts, finding yourself haunted by the faces of long-dead artisans and craftsmen and artists, spooked by the notion of hands creating these objects, fingers that had long since turned to skeleton, to dust. But never forgotten, never quite forgotten, not so long as you existed with your irrational passion.

For a moment the old feelings came back to him, assailed him, the first excitement he'd ever felt as a student. When? Fifteen years ago? sixteen? twenty? It didn't matter: time meant something different to him than it did to most people. Time was a thing you discovered through the secrets it had buried—in temples, in ruins, under rocks and dust and sand. Time expanded, became elastic, creating that amazing sense of everything that had ever lived being linked to everything that existed in the now; and death was fundamentally meaningless because of what you left behind.

Meaningless.

He thought of Champollion laboring over the Rosetta stone, the astonishment at finally deciphering ancient hieroglyphics. He thought of Schliemann finding the site of Troy. Flinders Petrie excavating the pre-dynastic cemetery at Nagada. Woolley discovering the royal cemetery at Ur in Iraq. Carter and Lord Carnarvon stumbling over the tomb of Tutankhamon.

That was where it had all begun. In that consciousness of discovery, which was like the eye of an intellectual hurricane. And you were swept along, carried away, transported backward in the kind of time machine the writers of fantasy couldn't comprehend: your personal time machine, your private line to the vital past.

He balanced the replica of the idol in the center of his hand and stared at it as if it were a personal enemy. No, he thought: you're your own worst enemy, Jones. You got carried away because you had access to half of a map among Forrestal's papers—and because you desperately wanted to trust two thugs who had the other half.

Moron, he thought.

And Belloq. Belloq was probably the smart one. Belloq had a razor-blade eye for the quick chance. Belloq always had had that quality—like the snakes you have a phobia about. Coming out unseen from under a rock, the slithering predator, always grasping for the thing he hasn't hunted for himself.

All that formed in the center of his mind now was an image of Belloq—that slender, handsome face, the dark of the eye, the smile that concealed the cunning.

He remembered other encounters with the Frenchman. He remembered graduate school, when Belloq had chiseled his way to the Archaeological Society Prize by presenting a paper on stratigraphy—the basis of which Indy recognized as being his own work. And in some way Belloq had plagiarized it, in some way he had found access to it. Indy couldn't prove anything because it would have been a case of sour grapes, a rash of envy.

1934. Remember the summer of that year, he thought.

1934. Black summer. He had spent months planning a dig in the Rub al Khali Desert of Saudi Arabia. Months of labor and preparation and scrounging for funds, putting the pieces together, arguing that his instincts about the dig were correct, that there were the remains of a nomadic culture to be found in that arid place, a culture pre-dating Christ. And then what?

He closed his eyes.

Even now the memory filled him with bitterness.

Belloq had been there before him.

Belloq had excavated the place.

It was true the Frenchman had found little of historic significance in the excavations, but that wasn't the point.

The point was that Belloq had stolen from him again. And again he wasn't sure how he could prove the theft.

And now the idol.

Indy looked up, startled out of his reverie, as the door of his office opened slowly.

Marcus Brody appeared, an expression of caution on his face, a caution that was in part concern. Indy considered Marcus, curator of the National Museum, his closest friend.

"Indiana," he said and his voice was soft.

He held the replica of the idol out, as if he were offering it to the other man, then he dropped it abruptly in the trash can on the floor.

"I had the real thing in my hand, Marcus. The real thing." Indy sat back, eyes shut, fingers vigorously massaging his eyelids.

"You told me, Indiana. You already told me," Brody said. "As soon as you came back. Remember?"

"I can get it back, Marcus. I can get it back. I figured it out. Belloq has to sell it, right? So where's he going to sell it? Huh?"

Brody looked tolerantly at him. "Where, Indiana?"

"Marrakesh. Marrakesh, that's where." Indy got up, indicating various figures that were on the desk. These were the items he'd taken from the Temple, the bits and pieces he'd swept up quickly. "Look. They've got to be worth something, Marcus. They've got to be worth enough money to get me to Marrakesh, right?"

Brody barely glanced at the items. Instead, he put out his hand and laid it on Indy's shoulder, a touch of friendship and concern. "The museum will buy them, as usual. No questions asked. But we'll talk about the idol later. Right now I want you to meet some people. They've come a long way to see you, Indiana."

"What people?"

Brody said, "They've come from Washington, Indiana. Just to see you."

"Who are they?" Indy asked wanly.

"Army Intelligence."

"Army *what?* Am I in some kind of trouble?"

"No. Quite the opposite, it would seem. They appear to need your help."

"The only help I'm interested in is getting the cash

together for Marrakesh, Marcus. These things have to be worth *something*."

"Later, Indiana. Later. First I want you to see these people."

Indy paused by the wall map of South America. "Yeah," he said. "I'll see them. I'll see them, if it means so much to you."

"They're waiting in the lecture hall."

They moved into the corridor.

A pretty young girl appeared in front of Indy. She was carrying a bundle of books and was pretending to look studious, efficient. Indy brightened when he saw her.

"Professor Jones," she was saying.

"Uh—"

"I was hoping we could have a conference," she said shyly, glancing at Marcus Brody.

"Yeah, sure, sure, Susan, I know I said we'd talk."

Marcus Brody said, "Not now. Not now, Indiana." And he turned to the girl. "Professor Jones has an *important* conference to attend, my dear. Why don't you call him later?"

"Yeah," Indy mumbled. "I'll be back at noon."

The girl smiled in a disappointed way, then drifted off along the corridor. Indy watched her go, admiring her legs, the roundness of the calves, the slender ankles. He felt Brody tug at his sleeve.

"Pretty. Up to your usual standards, Indiana. But later. Okay?"

"Later," Indy said, looking reluctantly away from the girl.

Brody pushed open the door of the lecture hall. Seated near the podium were two uniformed Army officers. They turned their faces in unison as the door opened.

"If this is the draft board, I've already served," Indy said.

Marcus Brody ushered Indy to a chair on the podium. "Indiana, I'd like to introduce you to Colonel Musgrove and Major Eaton. These are the people who've come from Washington to see you."

Eaton said, "Good to meet you. We've heard a lot about you, Professor Jones. Doctor of Archaeology, expert on the occult, obtainer of rare antiquities."

"That's one way to put it," Indy said.

"The 'obtainer of rare antiquities' sounds intriguing," the major said.

Indy glanced at Brody, who said, "I'm sure everything Professor Jones does for our museum here confirms strictly to the guidelines of the International Treaty for the Protection of Antiquities."

"Oh, I'm sure," Major Eaton said.

Musgrove said, "You're a man of many talents, Professor."

Indy made a dismissive gesture, waving a hand. What did these guys want?

Major Eaton said, "I understand you studied under Professor Ravenwood at the University of Chicago?"

"Yes."

"Have you any idea of his present whereabouts?"

Ravenwood. The name threw memories back with a kind of violence Indy didn't like. "Rumors, nothing more. I heard he was in Asia, I guess. I don't know."

"We understood you were pretty close to him," Musgrove said.

"Yeah." Indy rubbed his chin. "We were friends . . . We haven't spoken in years, though. I'm afraid we had what you might call a falling out." *A falling out,* he thought. There was a polite way to put it. A falling out—it was more like a total collapse. And then he was thinking of Marion, an unwanted memory, something he had yet to excavate from the deeper strata of his mind. Marion Ravenwood, the girl with the wonderful eyes.

Now the officers were whispering together, deciding something. Then Eaton turned and looked solemn and said, "What we're going to tell you has to remain confidential."

"Sure," Indy said. Ravenwood—where did the old man fit in all this fragile conundrum? And when was somebody going to get to the point?

Musgrove said, "Yesterday, one of our European

stations intercepted a German communiqué sent from Cairo to Berlin. The news in it was obviously exciting to the German agents in Egypt." Musgrove looked at Eaton, waiting for him to continue the narrative, as if each was capable of delivering only a certain amount of information at any one time.

Eaton said, "I'm not sure if I'm telling you something you already know, Professor Jones, when I mention the fact that the Nazis have had teams of archaeologists running around the world for the last two years—"

"It hasn't escaped my attention."

"Sure. They appear to be on a frantic search for any kind of religious artifact they can get. Hitler, according to our intelligence reports, is obsessed with the occult. We understand he even has a personal soothsayer, if that's the word. And right now it seems that some kind of archaeological dig—highly secretive—is going on in the desert outside Cairo."

Indy nodded. This was sending him to sleep. He knew of Hitler's seemingly endless concern with divining the future, making gold out of lead, hunting the elixir, whatever. You name it, he thought, and if it's weird enough, then the crazy little man with the mustache is sure to be interested in it.

Indy watched Musgrove take a sheet from his briefcase. He held it a moment, then he said, "This communiqué contains some information concerning the activity in the desert, but we don't know what to make of it. We thought it might mean something to you." And he passed the sheet to Indy. The message said:

TANIS DEVELOPMENT PROCEEDING.
ACQUIRE HEADPIECE, STAFF OF RA, ABNER
RAVENWOOD, US.

He read the words again, his mind suddenly clear, suddenly sharp. He stood up, looked at Brody and said, incredulously, "The Nazis have discovered Tanis."

Brody's face was grim and pale.

Eaton said, "Sorry. You've just lost me. What does Tanis mean to you?"

Indy walked from the podium to the window, his mind racing now. He pushed the window open and breathed in the crisp morning air, feeling it pleasingly cold in his lungs. *Tanis. The Staff of Ra. Ravenwood.* It flooded back to him now, the old legends, the fables, the stories. He was struck by a barrage of knowledge, information he'd stored in his brain for years—so much that he wanted to get it out quickly, speed through it. Take it slow, he thought. Tell it to them slowly so they'll understand. He turned to the officers and said, "A lot of this is going to be hard for you to understand. Maybe. I don't know. It's going to depend on your personal beliefs, I can tell you that much from the outset. Okay?" He paused, looking at their blank faces. "The city of Tanis is one of the possible resting places of the lost Ark."

Musgrove interrupted: "Ark? As in Noah?"

Indy shook his head. "Not Noah. I'm talking about the Ark of the Covenant. I'm talking about the chest the Israelites used to carry around the Ten Commandments."

Eaton said, "Back up. You mean *the* Ten Commandments?"

"I mean the *actual stone tablets,* the original ones Moses brought down from Mount Horeb. The ones he's said to have smashed when he saw the decadence of the Jews. While he was up in the mountain communing with God and being shown the law, the rest of his people are having orgies and building idols. So he's pretty angry and he breaks the tablets, right?"

The faces of the military men were impassive. Indy wished he could imbue them with the kind of enthusiasm he was beginning to feel himself.

"Then the Israelites put the broken pieces in the Ark and they carried it with them everywhere they went. When they settled in Canaan, the Ark was placed in the Temple of Solomon. It stayed there for years . . . then it was gone."

"Where?" Musgrove asked.

"Nobody knows who took it or when."

Brody, speaking more patiently than Indy, said, "An Egyptian pharaoh invaded Jerusalem around 926 B.C. Shishak by name. He *may* have taken it back to the city of Tanis—"

Indy cut in: "Where he may have hidden it in a secret chamber they called the Well of the Souls."

There was a silence in the hall.

Then Indy said, "Anyway, that's the myth. But bad things always seemed to happen to outsiders who meddled with the Ark. Soon after Shishak returned to Egypt, the city of Tanis was consumed by the desert in a sandstorm that lasted a year."

"The obligatory curse," Eaton said.

Indy was annoyed by the man's skepticism. "If you like," he said, trying to be patient. "But during the Battle of Jericho, Hebrew priests carried the Ark around the city for seven days before the walls collapsed. And when the Philistines supposedly captured the Ark, they brought the whole shooting works down on themselves—including plagues of boils and plagues of mice."

Eaton said, "This is all very interesting, I guess. But why would an American be mentioned in a Nazi cable, if we can get back to the point?"

"He's *the* expert on Tanis," Indy said. "Tanis was his obsession. He even collected some of its relics. But he never found the city."

"Why would the Nazis be interested in him?" Musgrove asked.

Indy paused for a moment. "It seems to me that the Nazis are looking for the headpiece to the Staff of Ra. And they think Abner has it."

"The Staff of Ra," Eaton said. "It's all somewhat farfetched."

Musgrove, who seemed more interested, leaned forward in his seat. "What is the Staff of Ra, Professor Jones?"

"I'll draw you a picture," Indy said. He strode to the blackboard and began to sketch quickly. As he drew the chalk across the board, he said, "The Staff of Ra is supposedly the clue to the location of the Ark. A pretty clever clue into the bargain. It was basically a long stick, maybe six feet high, nobody's really sure. Anyhow, it was capped by an elaborate headpiece in the shape of the sun, with a crystal at its center. You still with me? You had to take the staff to a special map room in the city of Tanis—it had the whole city laid out in miniature. When you placed the staff in a certain spot in this room at a certain time of day, the sun would shine through the crystal in the headpiece and send down a beam of light to the map, giving you the location of the Well of the Souls—"

"Where the Ark was concealed," Musgrove said.

"Right. Which is probably why the Nazis want the headpiece. Which explains Ravenwood's name in the cable."

Eaton got up and began moving around restlessly. "What does this Ark look like, anyhow?"

"I'll show you," Indy said. He went quickly to the back of the hall, found a book, flipped the pages until he came to a large color print. He showed it to the two military officers. They stared in silence at the illustration, which depicted a biblical battle scene. The army of the Israelites was vanquishing its foe; at the forefront of the Israelite ranks were two men carrying the Ark of the Covenant, an oblong gold chest with two golden cherubim crowning it. The Israelites carried the chest by poles placed through special rings in the corners. A thing of quite extraordinary beauty —but more impressive than its appearance was the piercing and brilliant jet of white light and flame that issued from the wings of the angels, a jet that drove into the ranks of the retreating army, creating apparent terror and devastation.

Impressed, Musgrove said, "What's that supposed to be coming out of the wings?"

Indy shrugged. "Who knows? Lightning. Fire. The power of God. Whatever you call it, it was supposedly capable of leveling mountains and wasting entire regions. According to Moses, an army that carried the

Ark before it was invincible." Indy looked at Eaton's face and decided, This guy has no imagination. Nothing will ever set this character on fire. Eaton shrugged and continued to stare at the illustration. Disbelief, Indy thought. Military skepticism.

Musgrove said, "What are your own feelings about this . . . so-called power of the Ark, Professor?"

"As I said, it depends on your beliefs. It depends on whether you accept the myth as having some basis in truth."

"You're sidestepping," Musgrove said and smiled.

"I keep an open mind," Indy answered.

Eaton turned away from the picture. "A nut like Hitler, though . . . He might really believe in this power, right? He might buy the whole thing."

"Probably," Indy said. He watched Eaton a moment, suddenly feeling a familiar sense of anticipation, a rise in his temperature. *The lost city of Tanis. The Well of the Souls. The Ark.* There was an elusive melody here, and it enticed him like the seductive call of a siren.

"He might imagine that with the Ark his military machine would be invincible," Eaton said, more to himself than to anybody else. "I can see, if he swallows the whole fairy tale, the psychological advantage he'd feel at the very least."

Indy said, "There's one other thing. According to legend, the Ark will be recovered at the time of the coming of the true Messiah."

"The true Messiah," Musgrove said.

"Which is what Hitler probably imagines himself to be," Eaton remarked.

There was a silence in the hall now. Indy looked once more at the illustration, the savagery of the light that flashed from the wings of the angels and scorched the retreating enemies. A power beyond all power. Beyond definition. He shut his eyes for a second. What if it *was* true? What if such a power *did* exist? Okay, you try to be rational, you try to work it like Eaton, putting it down to some old fable, something circulated by a bunch of zealous Israelites.

A scare tactic against their enemies, a kind of psychological warfare even. Just the same, there was something here you couldn't ignore, couldn't shove aside.

He opened his eyes and heard Musgrove sigh and say, "You've been very helpful. I hope we can call on you again if we need to."

"Anytime, gentlemen. Anytime you like," Indy said.

There was a round of handshakes, then Brody escorted the officers to the door. Alone in the empty hall, Indy closed the book. He thought for a moment, trying at the same time to suppress the sense of excitement he felt. *The Nazis have found Tanis*—and these words went around and around in his brain.

The girl, Susan, said, "I really hope I didn't embarrass you when you were with Brody. I mean, I was so . . . obvious."

"You weren't obvious," Indy said.

They were sitting together in the cluttered living room of Indy's small frame house. The room was filled with souvenirs of trips, of digs, restored clay vessels and tiny statues and fragments of pottery and maps and globes—as cluttered, he sometimes thought, as my life.

The girl drew her knees up, hugging them, laying her face down against them. Like a cat, he thought. A tiny contented cat.

"I love this room," she said. "I love the whole house . . . but this room especially."

Indy got up from the sofa and, hands in his pockets, walked around the room. The girl, for some reason, was more of an intrusion than she should have been. Sometimes when she spoke he tuned her out. He heard only the noise of her voice and not the meaning of her words. He poured himself a drink, sipped it, swallowed; it burned in his chest—a good burning, like a small sun glowing down there.

Susan said, "You seem so distant tonight, Indy."

"Distant?"

"You've got something on your mind. I don't know." She shrugged.

He walked to the radio, turned it on, barely listening to the drone of someone making a pitch for Maxwell House. The girl changed the station and then there was dance-band music. Distant, he thought. Farther than you could dream. Miles away. Oceans and continents and centuries. He was suddenly thinking about Ravenwood, about the last conversation they'd had, the old man's terrible storm, his wrath. When he listened to the echoes of those voices, he felt sad, disappointed in himself; he'd taken some fragile trust and shattered it.

Marion's infatuated with you, and you took advantage of that.

You're twenty-eight, presumably a grown man, and you've taken advantage of a young girl's brainless infatuation and twisted it to suit your own purpose just because she thinks she's in love with you.

Susan said, "If you want me to leave, Indy, I will. If you want to be alone, I'll understand."

"It's okay. Really. Stay."

There was a knock on the door; the porch creaked.

Indy moved out of the living room along the hallway and saw Marcus Brody outside. He was smiling a secretive smile, as if he had news he wanted to linger over, savor for as long as he could.

"Marcus," Indy said. "I wasn't expecting you."

"I think you were," Brody said, pushing the screen door.

"We'll go in the study," Indy said.

"What's wrong with the living room?"

"Company."

"Ah. What else?"

They entered the study.

"You did it, didn't you?" Indy said.

Brody smiled. "They want you to get the Ark before the Nazis."

It was a moment before Indy could say anything. He felt a sense of exaltation, an awareness of triumph. *The Ark.* He said, "I think I've been waiting all my life to hear something like that."

Brody looked at the shot glass in Indy's hand for a moment. "They talked with their people in Washington. Then they consulted me. They want you, Indiana. They want *you.*"

Indy sat down behind his desk, gazed into his glass, then looked around the room. A strange emotion filled him suddenly; this was more than books and articles and maps, more than speculation, scholarly argument, discussion, debate—a sense of reality had replaced all the words and pictures.

Brody said, "Of course, given the military mind, they don't exactly buy all that business about the power of the Ark and so forth. They don't want to embrace any such mythologies. After all, they're soldiers, and soldiers like to think they're hard-line realists. They want the Ark—and I'll quote, if I can —because of its 'historic and cultural significance' and because 'such a priceless object should not become the property of a fascist regime.' Or words to that effect."

"Their reasons don't matter," Indy said.

"In addition, they'll pay handsomely—"

"I don't care about the money, either, Marcus." Indy raised a hand, indicated the room in a sweep. "The Ark represents the elusive thing I feel about archaeology—you know, history concealing its secrets. Things lying out there waiting to be discovered. I don't give *that* for their reasons or their money." And he snapped his fingers.

Brody nodded his head in understanding. "The museum, of course, will get the Ark."

"Of course."

"If it exists . . ." Brody paused a moment, then added, "We shouldn't build our hopes up too high."

Indy stood up. "I have to find Abner first. That would be the logical step. If Abner has the headpiece, then I have to get it before the opposition does. That makes sense, right? Without the headpiece, *voilà,* no Ark. So where do I find Abner?" He stopped, realizing how quickly he'd been talking. "I think I know where to start looking—"

Brody said, "It's been a long time, Indiana. Things change."

Indy stared at the other man for a second. The comment was enigmatic to him: *Things change*. And then he realized Marcus Brody was talking about Marion.

"He might have mellowed toward you," Brody said. "On the other hand, he might still carry a grudge. In that case, it's reasonable to assume he wouldn't want to give you the headpiece. If in fact he has it."

"We'll hope for the best, my friend."

"Always the optimist, right?"

"Not always," Indy said. "Optimism can be deadly."

Brody was silent now, moving around the room, flicking the pages of books. Then he looked at Indy in a somber way. "I want you to be careful, Indiana."

"I'm always careful."

"You can be pretty reckless. I know that as well as you. But the Ark isn't like anything you've gone after before. It's bigger. More dangerous." Brody slammed a book shut, as if to emphasize a point. "I'm not skeptical, like those military people—I think the Ark has secrets. I think it has dangerous secrets."

For a second Indy was about to say something flippant, something about the melodramatic tone in the other man's voice. But he saw from the expression on Brody's face that the man was serious.

"I don't want to lose you, Indiana, no matter how great the prize is. You understand?"

The two men shook hands.

Indy noticed that Brody's skin was damp with sweat.

Alone, Indy sat up late into the night, unable to sleep, unable to let his mind rest. He wandered from one room of the small house to another, clenching and unclenching his hands. After all these years, he thought, all this passage of time—would Ravenwood help him? Would Ravenwood, given that he had the headpiece, come to his assistance? And behind these questions there lingered still another one. Would Marion still be with her father?

He continued to go from room to room until finally he settled in his study and put his feet up on the desk, looking at the various objects stuffed in the room. Then he closed his eyes for a moment, tried to think clearly, and rose. From a bookshelf he removed a copy of Ravenwood's old journal, a gift from the old man when the two were still friends. Indy skimmed the pages, noticing one disappointment listed after another, one excavation that hadn't lived up to its promises, another that had revealed only the most slender, the most tantalizing, of clues to the whereabouts of the Ark. The outlines of an obsession in these pages; the heartbreaking search for a lost object of history. But the Ark could flow in your blood and fill the air you breathed. And he understood the old man's single-mindedness, his devotion, the kind of lust that had led him from one country to another, to one hope after another. The pages yielded up that much—but there was no mention of the headpiece anywhere. Nothing.

The last item in the journal mentioned the country of Nepal, the prospect of another dig. Nepal, Indy thought: the Himalayas, the roughest terrain on earth. And a long way from whatever the Germans were doing in Egypt. Maybe Ravenwood had stumbled onto something else back then, a fresh clue to the Ark. Maybe all the old stuff about Tanis was incorrect. Just maybe.

Nepal. It was a place in which to start.

It was a beginning.

He fingered the journal a moment longer, then he set it down, wishing he knew how Abner Ravenwood would react to him.

And how Marion would respond.

4: Berchtesgaden, Germany

Dietrich was uneasy in the company of René Belloq. It wasn't so much the lack of trust he felt in the Frenchman, the feeling he had that Belloq treated almost everything with equal cynicism; it was, rather, the strange charisma of Belloq that worried Dietrich, the idea that somehow you *wanted* to like him, that he was drawing you in despite yourself.

They were seated together in an anteroom at Berchtesgaden, the Führer's mountain retreat, a place Dietrich had never visited before and which filled him with some awe. But he noticed that Belloq, lounging casually, his long legs outstretched, gave no sign of any similar feeling. Quite the opposite—Belloq might have been sitting sprawled in a cheap French café, in fact in the kind of place where Dietrich had found him in Marseilles. No respect, Dietrich thought. No sense of the importance of things. He was irritated by the archaeologist's attitude.

He listened to a clock tick, the delicate sounds of chimes. Belloq sighed, shifted his legs around and looked at his wristwatch.

"What are we waiting for, Dietrich?" he asked.

Dietrich couldn't help talking in a low voice.

"The Führer will see us when he's ready, Belloq. You must think he has nothing better to do than spend his time speaking to you about some museum piece."

"A museum piece." Belloq spoke with obvious contempt, staring across the room at the German. How little they know, he thought. How little they understand of history. They put their faith in all the wrong things: they build their monumental arches and parade their strutting armies—failing to realize you cannot deliberately create the awe of history. It is something that already exists, something you cannot aspire to fabricate with the trappings of grandeur. The Ark: the very thought of the possibility of discovering the Ark made him impatient. Why did he have to speak with this miserable little German house painter, anyhow? Why was he obliged to sit through a meeting with the man when the dig had already begun in Egypt? What, after all, could he learn from Hitler? Nothing, he thought. Absolutely nothing. Some pompous lecture, perhaps. A diatribe of some kind. Something about the greatness of the Reich. About how, if the Ark existed, it belonged in Germany.

What did any of them know? he wondered.

The Ark didn't belong anywhere. If it had secrets, if it contained the kind of power it was said to, then he wanted to be the first to discover it—it wasn't something to be lightly entrusted to the maniac who sat, even now, in some other room of this mountain lodge and kept him waiting.

He sighed impatiently, shifting in his chair.

And then he got up, walked to the window and looked out across the mountains, not really seeing them, noticing them only in an absent way. He was thinking of the moment of opening the box, looking inside and seeing the relics of the stone tablets Moses had brought down from Mount Horeb. It was easy to imagine his hand raising the lid, the sound of his own voice—then the moment of revelation.

The moment of a lifetime: there was no prize greater than the Ark of the Covenant.

When he turned from the window, Dietrich was watching him. The German noticed the odd look in Belloq's eyes, the faint smile on the mouth that seemed to be directed inward, as if he were enjoying an immensely private joke, some deep and amusing thought. He realized then how far his own lack of trust went—but this was the Führer's affair, it was the Führer who had asked for the best, the Führer who had asked for René Belloq.

Dietrich heard the clock chime the quarter hour. From a corridor somewhere inside the building, he heard the sound of footsteps. Belloq turned expectantly toward the door. But the footsteps faded and Belloq cursed quietly in French.

"How much longer are we supposed to wait?" the Frenchman asked.

Dietrich shrugged.

"Don't tell me," Belloq said. "The Führer lives his life by a clock to which we ordinary men have no access, correct? Perhaps he has visions of his own private time, no? Perhaps he thinks he has some profound knowledge of the nature of time?" Belloq made a gesture of despair with one hand, then he smiled.

Dietrich moved uncomfortably, beset by the notion that the room was wired, that Hitler was listening to this insane talk. He said, "Does nothing awe you, Belloq?"

"I might answer you, Dietrich, except I doubt you would understand what I was talking about."

They were silent now. Belloq returned to the window. Every moment stuck here is a moment less to spend in Egypt, he thought. And he realized that time was important, that news of the dig would spread, that it couldn't be kept secret forever. He only hoped that German security was good.

He looked at the German again and said, "You haven't fully explained to me, as a matter of interest, how the headpiece is to be obtained. I need to know."

"It is being taken care of," Dietrich said. "People have been sent—"

"What kind of people, Dietrich? Is there an archaeologist among them?"

"Why, no—"

"Thugs, Dietrich? Some of your bullies?"

"Professionals."

"Ah, but not professional archaeologists. How are they to know if they discover the headpiece? How are they supposed to know it isn't a forgery?"

Dietrich smiled. "The secret lies in knowing *where* to look, Belloq. It doesn't entirely depend on knowing *what* you're looking for."

"A man like Ravenwood is not easily coerced," Belloq said.

"Did I mention coercion?"

"You didn't have to," Belloq said. "I appreciate the need for it, which is enough. In certain areas, I think you'll find that I am not a squeamish man. In fact, if I say so myself, quite the opposite."

Dietrich nodded. Again there were footsteps outside the door. He waited. The door was opened. A uniformed aide, dressed in that black tunic Dietrich so disliked, stepped inside. He said nothing, merely indicated with a backward nod of his head that they were to follow him.

Belloq moved toward the door. The inner shrine, he thought. The sanctum of the little house painter who has dreams of being the spirit of history but who fails to realize the truth. The only history in which Belloq was interested, the only history that made any sense, lay buried in the deserts of Egypt. With luck, Belloq thought. With any luck.

He saw Dietrich move ahead. A nervous man, his face as pale as that of someone stepping, with as much dignity as he can muster, to his own execution.

The thought amused Belloq.

5: Nepal

The DC-3 cruised over the white slopes of the mountains, skimming now and then through walls of mist, banks of dense cloud. The peaks of the range were mostly invisible, hidden in the frosty clouds, clouds that seemed motionless and solid, as if no wintry wind could ever disperse them.

A devious route, Indy thought, staring out his window, and a long one: across the United States to San Francisco, then Pan Am's China Clipper, arriving after many stops in Hong Kong; another rickety plane to Shanghai, and finally this aging machine to Katmandu.

Indy shivered as he imagined the frigid bleakness of the Himalayas. The impossible crags, the unmapped gulleys and valleys, the thick snow that covered everything. An inconceivable environment, and yet life flourished here, people survived, labored, loved. He shut the book he'd been reading—the journal of Abner Ravenwood—and he looked along the aisle of the plane. He put his hand in the back pocket of his jacket and felt the wad of money there, what Marcus Brody had called "an advance from the U.S. military." He had more than five thousand dollars, which he'd begun to think of as persuasion money if Abner Ravenwood hadn't changed in his attitude toward him. A touch of bribery, of *la mordida.* Presumably the old man would be in need of money, since he hadn't held any official teaching post, so far as Indy knew, in years. He would have gone through that great scourge of any academic discipline—the pain of finding funds. The begging bowl you were obliged to rattle all the time. Five grand, Indy realized, was more money than he'd ever carried at any one time. A small fortune, in fact. And it made him feel decidedly uncomfortable. He'd never had more than a cavalier attitude toward money, spending it as quickly as he made it.

For a time he shut his eyes, wondering if he would find Marion with her father still. No, it wasn't likely, he decided. She would have grown up, drifted away, maybe even married back in the States. On the other hand, what if she was still with her father? What then? And he found himself suddenly unwilling to look Ravenwood in the eye.

All those years, though. Surely things would have changed.

Maybe not, maybe not with somebody as single-minded as Abner. A grudge was a grudge—and if a colleague had an affair with your daughter, your child, then the grudge would be long and hard. Indy sighed. A weakness, he thought. Why couldn't you have been strong back then? Why did you have to get so carried away? So involved with a kid? But then, she hadn't seemed like a kid, more a child-woman, something in her eyes and her look suggesting more than a girl going through adolescence.

Drop it, forget it, he thought.

You have other things on your mind now. And Nepal is just one step on the way to Egypt.

One long step.

Indy felt the plane begin to drop almost imperceptibly at first, then noticeably, as it ploughed downward toward its landing spot. He could see emerging from the snowy wastes the thin lights of a town. He shut his eyes and waited for that moment when the wheels struck ground and the plane screamed along the runway as it braked. Then the plane was taxiing toward a terminal building—no more than a large hangar that had apparently been converted into an arrivals-and-departures point. He got up from his seat, collected his papers and books, took his bag from beneath the seat and began to move down the aisle.

Indiana Jones didn't notice the raincoated man just behind him. A passenger who had embarked in Shanghai and who, throughout the last part of the journey, had been watching him down the aisle.

The wind that ripped across the airfield was biting, piercing through Indy. He bent his head and hurried toward the hangar, holding his old felt hat in place with one hand, the canvas bag in the other. And then he was in the building, where it wasn't much warmer, the only heat seeming to be that of the massed bodies crammed inside the place. He quickly passed through the formalities of customs, but then he was thronged by beggars, children with lame legs, blind kids, a couple of palsied men, a few withered humans whose sex he couldn't determine. They clutched at him, imploring him, but since he knew the nature of beggars from other parts of the world, he also knew it was best to avoid dispensing gifts. He brushed past them, amazed by the activity inside the place. It was as much a bazaar as an airport building, stuffed with stalls, animals, the wild activity of the marketplace. Men burned sweetbreads over braziers, others gambled excitedly over a form of dice, still others seemed involved in an auction of donkeys—the creatures were tethered miserably together in a line, skin and bone, dull eyes and ragged fur. Still the beggars pursued him. He moved more quickly now, past the stalls that belonged to moneychangers, to vendors selling items of unrecognizable fruits and vegetables, past the merchants of rugs and scarves and clothing made from the hide of the yak, past the primitive food-stands and the cold-drink places, assailed all the time by smells, by the scent of burning grease, the whiff of perfume, the aromas of weird spices. He heard someone call his name through the crowd and Indy paused, swinging his canvas bag lightly to warn the beggars off. He stared in the direction of the voice. He saw the face of Lin-Su, still familiar even after so many years. He reached the small Chinese man and they shook hands vigorously. Lin-Su, his wrinkled face broken into a smile that was almost entirely toothless, took Indy by the elbow and escorted him through a doorway and out onto the street—where the wind, a savage, demented thing, came howling out of the mountains and scoured the street as if it were bent on an old vengeance. They moved into a doorway, the small Chinese still holding Indy by the arm.

"I am glad to see you again," Lin-Su said in an English that was both quaint and measured, and rusty from lack of use. "It has been many years."

"Too many," Indy said. "Twelve? Thirteen?"

"As you say, twelve . . ." Lin-Su paused and looked along the street. "I received your cable, of course." His voice faded as his attention was drawn to a movement in the street, a shadow crossing a doorway. "You will pardon this question, my old friend: Is somebody following you?"

Indy looked puzzled. "Nobody I'm aware of."

"No matter. The eyes create trickery."

Indy glanced down the street. He didn't see anything other than the shuttered fronts of small shops and a pale light the color of a kerosene flame falling from the open doorway of a coffeehouse.

The small Chinese hesitated for a moment, then said, "I have made inquiries for you, as you asked me to."

"And?"

"It is hard in a country like this to obtain information quickly. This you understand. The lack of lines of communication. And the weather, of course. The accursed snow makes it difficult. The telephone system is primitive, where it exists, that is." Lin-Su laughed. "However, I can tell you that the last time Abner Ravenwood was heard from, he was in the region around Patan. This much I can vouch for. Everything else I have learned is rumor and hardly worth discussion."

"Patan, huh? How long ago?"

"That is hard to say. Reliably, three years ago." Lin-Su shrugged. "I am very apologetic I can do no better, my friend."

"You've done very well," Indy said. "Is there a chance he might still be there?"

"I can tell you that nobody had any knowledge of him leaving this country. Beyond that . . ." Lin-Su shivered and turned up the collar of his heavy coat.

"It helps," Indy said.

"I wish it could be more, naturally. I have not forgotten the assistance you gave me when I was last in your great country."

"All I did was intervene with the Immigration Service, Lin-Su."

"So. But you informed them that I was employed at your museum when in fact I was not."

"A white lie," Indy said.

"And what is friendship but the sum of favors?"

"As you say," Indy remarked. He wasn't always comfortable with Oriental platitudes, those kinds of comments that might have been lifted from the writings of a third-rate Confucius. But he understood that Lin-Su's Chinese act was performed almost professionally, as if he were speaking the way Occidentals expected him to.

"How do I get to Patan?"

Lin-Su raised one finger in the air. "There I can help you. In fact, I have already taken the liberty. Come this way."

Indy followed the little man some way down the street. Parked against a building there was a black car of an unfamiliar kind. Lin-Su indicated it with pride.

"At your disposal I place my automobile."

"Are you sure?"

"Indeed. Inside you will find the necessary map."

"I'm overwhelmed."

"A small matter," Lin-Su said.

Indy walked round the car. He glanced through the window and looked at the broken leather upholstery and the appearance of springs.

"What make is it?" he asked.

"A mongrel breed, I fear," Lin-Su said. "It has been put together by a mechanic in China and shipped to me at some expense. It is part Ford, part Citroën. I think there may be elements of a Morris, too."

"How the hell do you get it repaired?"

"That I can answer. I have my fingers crossed it never breaks down." The Chinese laughed and handed a set of keys to Indy. "And so far it has been reliable. Which is good, because the roads are extremely bad."

"Tell me about the roads to Patan."

"Bad. However, with any luck you will avoid the snows. Follow the route I have marked in the map. You should be safe."

"I can't thank you enough," Indy said.

"You will not stay the night?"

"I'm afraid not."

Lin-Su smiled. "You have . . . what is that word? Ah, yes. A deadline?"

"Right. I have a deadline."

"Americans," he said. "They always have deadlines. And they always have ulcers."

"No ulcers yet," Indy said, and opened the car door. It creaked badly on its hinges.

"The clutch is stiff," Lin-Su said. "The steering is poor. But it will take you to your destination and bring you back again."

Indy threw his bag onto the passenger seat. "What more could a man ask from a car, huh?"

"Good luck, In-di-an-a." It was like a Chinese name, the way Lin-Su pronounced it.

They shook hands, then Indy pulled the car door shut. He turned the key in the ignition, listened to the engine whine, and then the car was going. He waved to the small Chinese, who was already moving down the street, beaming as if he were proud to have loaned his car to an American. Indy glanced at the map and hoped it was accurate because he sure couldn't expect highway signs in a place like this.

He drove for hours along the rutted roads Lin-Su had marked on the map, aware as darkness fell of the mountains looming like great spooks all around him. He was glad he couldn't see the various passes that swept down beneath him. Here and there where snow blocked the road he had to edge the car through slowly, sometimes getting out and scraping as much snow from his path as he could. A desolate place. Bleak beyond belief. Indy wondered about living here in what must seem an endless winter. The roof of the world, they said. And he could believe it, except it was a mighty lonesome roof. Lin-Su apparently could stand it, but then it was probably a good place for the Chinaman to have his business, the importing and exporting of lines of merchandise that were sometimes of a dubious nature. Nepal—it was where all the world's contraband came through, whether stolen objects of art, antiquities or narcotics. It was where the authorities turned eyes that were officially blind and forever had their palms held out to be slyly greased.

Through the margins of sleep Indy drove, yawning, wishing he had some coffee to keep him going. Mile after dreary mile he listened to the springs of the mongrel car creak and squeal, to the squelch of tires on the snow. And then unexpectedly, before he could check his destination on the map, he found himself on the outskirts of a town, a town that had no designation, no sign, no name. He pulled the car to the side of the road and opened the map. He switched on the interior light and realized he must have reached Patan because there wasn't any other sizable community marked on Lin-Su's map. He drove slowly through the straggling outskirts of the place, dismal huts, constructions of windowless clay shacks. And then he reached what looked like the main thoroughfare, a narrow street—little more than an alley—of tiny stores, passageways that led off at sinister angles into shadows. He stopped the car and looked around him. A strange street—too silent in some way.

Indy was suddenly conscious of another car cruising behind him. It passed, swerved as if to avoid him, picked up speed as it moved. When it disappeared he realized it was the only other car he'd seen all the way. What a godforsaken hole, he thought, trying to imagine Abner Ravenwood living here. How could anybody stand this?

Somebody moved along the street, coming toward him. A man, a large man in a fur jacket, who swayed from side to side like a drunk. Indy got out of the car and waited until the man in the fur jacket had come close to him before speaking. The man's breath smelled of booze, a smell so strong that Indy had to turn his face to the side.

The man, like somebody expecting to be attacked, stepped suspiciously away. Indy held his arms out, hands upturned, a gesture of harmlessness. But the man didn't come any closer. He watched Indy warily. A man of mixed heritage, the shape of the eyes suggesting the Orient, the broad cheekbones perhaps indicating some Slavic mix. Try a language, Indy thought. Try English for a start.

"I'm looking for Ravenwood," he said. This is absurd, he said to himself: the dead of night in some deserted place and you're looking for somebody in a language that probably makes no sense. "A man called Ravenwood."

The man stared, not understanding. He opened his mouth.

"Do. You. Know. Somebody. Called. Ravenwood?" Slowly. Like speaking with an idiot.

"Raven-wood?" the man said.

"You got it, chum," Indy said.

"Raven-wood." The man appeared to suck the word as though it were a lozenge of an exotic flavor.

"Yeah. Right. Now we stand here all night and mumble, I guess," Indy said, cold again, tiredness coursing through him.

"Ravenwood." The man smiled in recognition and

turned, pointing along the street. Indy looked and noticed a light in the distance. The man cupped one hand and raised it to his mouth, the gesture of a drinker. *"Ravenwood,"* he said over and over, still pointing. He began to nod his head vigorously. Indy understood he was to go in the direction of the light.

"Much obliged," he said.

"Ravenwood," the man said again.

"Yeah, right, right," and Indy moved back to the car.

He got in and drove along the street, stopped at the light the man had indicated, and only then realized it emerged from a tavern, outside of which, incongruously, hung a sign in English: THE RAVEN. The Raven, Indy thought. The guy had made a mistake. Confused and drunk, that was all. Still, if it was the only joint open in this hick burg, he could stop and see if anybody knew anything. He got out of the car, aware of the noise coming from inside the tavern now, the rabbling kind of noise created by any congregation of drinkers who've spent their last several hours devoted to the task of wasting themselves. It was a noise he enjoyed, one he was accustomed to, and he would have liked nothing better than to join the revelers inside. Uh-uh, he said to himself. You haven't come all this way to get loaded like a lost tourist checking the local lowlife. You've come with a purpose. A well-defined purpose.

He moved toward the door. You've been in some weird places in your time, he told himself. But this takes the blue ribbon for sure. What he saw in front of him as he stepped inside was an odd collection of boozers, a wild assortment of nationalities. It was as if somebody had picked up a scoop, dipped it into a jar filled with mixed ethnic types and spilled it here in the mad, lonely darkness of the wilderness. This one *really* takes the cake, Indy laughed to himself. Sherpa mountain guides, Nepalese natives, Mongols, Chinese, Indians, bearded mountain climbers who looked like they'd fall off a stepladder in their present condition, various furtive kinds of no obvious national origin.

This is Nepal, all right, he thought, and these are the drifters of the international narcotics trade, smugglers, bandits. Indy shut the door behind him, then noticed a huge stuffed raven, wings spread viciously, mounted behind the long bar. A sinister memento, he thought. And something troubled him, the odd similarity between the name of Abner and the name of this bar. Coincidence? He moved further into the room, which smelled of sweat and alcohol and tobacco smoke. He detected the sweet, aromatic scent of hashish in the air.

Something was going on at the bar, where most of the clientele was gathered. Some kind of drinking contest. Lined up on the bar was a collection of shot glasses. A large man, shouting in an Australian accent, was stumbling against the bar even as he raised his hand and blindly fumbled for his next drink.

Indy moved nearer. A drinking contest. And he wondered who the Australian's opponent might be. He pushed his way through, trying to get a look.

When he saw, when he recognized the opponent in the contest, he felt a moment of dizziness, a giddiness that was tight in his chest, a stab, a quick ache. And for a second the passage of time altered, changed like a landscape painted long ago and left untouched. An illusion. A mirage. And he shook his head as if this movement might bring him back to reality.

Marion.

Marion, he thought.

The dark hair that fell around her shoulders in loose, soft waves; the same large intelligent brown eyes that surveyed the world with a mild skepticism, an incredulity at what passed for human behavior—eyes that always appeared to look inside you, as if they might perceive your innermost motivation; the mouth—perhaps only the mouth was a little different, a little harder, and the body a little fuller. But it was Marion, the Marion of his memory.

And here she was involved in an insane drinking contest with a bear of an Australian. He watched, hardly daring to move, as the throng around the bar made bets on the contest. Even to the most innocent spectator, it must have seemed wildly unlikely that the Australian could be outdrunk by a woman barely more than a couple of inches over five feet tall. But she was throwing back drinks, matching the man glass for glass.

Something inside him, something that lay hard in the center of him, became suddenly soft. He wanted to drag her away from the lunacy of the place. No, he told himself. She's not a child anymore, she's not Abner's daughter now—she's a woman, a beautiful woman. And she knows what she's doing. She can take care of herself—here, even in the middle of this motley crew of burnt-out cases and bandits and boozers. She tossed down another drink. The crowd roared. More money was thrown down on the bar. Another roar. The Australian staggered back, reached for a drink, missed and toppled backward like an axed tree. Indy was impressed. He watched as she tossed her black hair back, picked up the money from the bar and shouted at the drinkers in Nepalese; and although he didn't know the language, it was obvious from her tone of voice she was telling them that their sport was over for the evening. But there was one glass left on the counter and they weren't going to move until she'd drunk it.

She stared around them, then she said, "Bums." And she drank the glass down. The crowd roared again, then Marion waved her arms in the air and the mob began to disperse, grumblingly, moving toward the door. The barman, a tall Nepalese character, was making sure they left, ushering them out into the night. He had an ax handle in one hand. In a joint like this, Indy thought, you might need more than an ax handle to ensure closing time.

Then the bar was empty, the last stragglers having gone out.

Marion went behind the bar, raised her face and looked at Indy.

"Hey, didn't you hear me? You deaf or something? Time's up. You understand? *Bairra chuh kayho?*"

She began to move toward him. And then, the light of recognition on her face, she paused.

"Hiya, Marion," he said.

She didn't move.

She simply stared at him.

He was trying to see her now as she was, not remember her as she had been, and the effort was suddenly difficult. He felt tight again, this time in his throat, as if something had congealed there.

"Hello, Marion," he said again. He sat down on a barstool.

For a second he imagined he saw some old emotion in her eyes, something locked there in her look—but then what she did next astonished him. She made a hard fist of her hand, swung her arm at great speed and struck him with a solid right to the side of his jaw. Dizzy, he fell from the stool and lay sprawled across the floor, looking up at her.

"Nice to see you, too," he said and, rubbing his jaw, grinned.

She said, "Get up and get out."

"Wait, Marion."

She stood over him. "I can do it a second time just as easy," she said, making a fist again.

"I bet," he said. He rose to his knees. The jaw was damn sore. Where had she learned to hit that way? Where had she learned to drink so well, come to think of it? *Surprise, surprise,* he thought. *The girl becomes a woman and the woman turns out to be a terror.*

"I don't have anything to say to you."

He rose now and rubbed dirt from his clothes. "Okay, okay," he said. "Maybe you don't want to talk to me. I can understand that—"

"That's insightful of you."

That bitterness, Indy thought. Did he deserve that bitterness? Yeah, maybe, he realized.

"I came to see your father," he said.

"You're two years too late."

Indy was aware of the Nepalese bartender nursing his ax handle. A menacing character altogether.

"It's okay, Mohan. I can handle this." She gestured contemptuously at Indy. "Go on home."

Mohan laid the ax handle on the bar. At her nod, he shrugged and left.

"What do you mean 'two years too late'?" Indy asked slowly. "What's happened to Abner?"

For the first time something in Marion softened. She exhaled slowly, breathing out an old sadness. "What do you think I mean? An avalanche got him. What else could get him? It's only fitting—he spent his whole damn life digging. As far as I know he's probably still up the side of that mountain, preserved in the snow."

She turned away from him and poured herself a drink. Indy sat down on the barstool again. *Abner dead.* It was inconceivable. He felt as if he'd been struck again.

"He became convinced his beloved Ark was parked halfway up some mountain." Marion sipped her drink. He could see some of her hardness, some of that exterior shell, begin to crack. But she was fighting it, fighting the display of weakness.

She said, "He dragged me, a kid, halfway round the world on his crazy digs. Then he pops off. He didn't leave me a penny. Guess how I lived, Jones? I worked here. And I wasn't exactly the bartender, you understand?"

Indy stared at her. He wondered what he was feeling now, what kind of strange sensations were moving inside him. They were unfamiliar to him, alien. She suddenly looked terribly fragile. And terribly beautiful.

"The guy that owned the place went crazy. *Everybody* goes crazy here sooner or later. So when they dragged him away, guess what? He leaves me this place. All mine for the rest of my natural. Can you imagine a worse curse?"

It was too much for Indy to absorb at once, too much to take in. He wanted to say something that might comfort her. But he knew there weren't any words.

"I'm sorry," he said.

"Big deal."

"I'm really sorry."

"I thought I was in love with you," she said. "And look what you did with that sacred piece of knowledge."

"I didn't mean to hurt you."

"I was a child!"

"Look, I did what I did. I'm not happy about it, I can't explain it. And I don't expect you to be happy about it, either."

"It was wrong, Indiana Jones. And you knew it was wrong."

Indy was silent, wondering how you could ever apologize for past events. "If I could go back ten years, if I could undo the whole damn thing, believe me, Marion, I would."

"I knew you'd come through that door sometime. Don't ask me why. I just knew it," she said.

He put his hands on the bar. "Why didn't you go back to the States, anyhow?" he asked.

"Money. Pure and simple. I want to go back in some kind of style," she said.

"Maybe I can help. Maybe I can start to do you some good."

"Is *that* why you came back?"

He shook his head. "I need one of the pieces that I think your father had."

Marion's right hand came up swiftly, but this time Indy was ready and caught her wrist.

"Sonofabitch," she said. "I wish you'd leave that crazy old man in peace. God knows you caused him enough heartache when he was alive."

"I'll pay," he said.

"How much?"

"Enough to get you back to the States in style, anyhow."

"Yeah? Trouble is, I sold all his stuff. Junk. All of it. He wasted his whole life on junk."

"Everything? You sold everything?"

"You look disappointed. How does *that* feel, Mr. Jones?"

Indy smiled at her. Her second of triumph pleased him in some way. And then he wondered if she was telling the truth about selling Abner's stuff, if it was all really so valueless.

"I like it when you look dejected," she said. "I'll buy you a drink. Name it."

"Seltzer," he said, and sighed.

"Seltzer, huh? Changed days, Indiana Jones. I prefer scotch myself. I like bourbon and vodka and gin, too. I'm not much for brandy. I'm off that."

"You're a tough broad now, aren't you?"

She smiled at him again. "This ain't exactly Schenectady, friend."

He rubbed his jaw once more. Suddenly he was tired of the fencing. "How many times can I say I'm sorry? Would it ever be enough?"

She pushed a glass of soda toward him and he drank from it with a grimace. Then she leaned against the bar, propped on her elbows. "You can pay cash money, can you?"

"Yeah."

"Tell me about this thing you're looking for. Who knows? Maybe I can locate the guy I sold the stuff to."

"A bronze piece in the shape of the sun. It has a hole in it, slightly off center. There's a red crystal in it. It comes from the top of a staff. Does it sound familiar?"

"Maybe. How much?"

"Three thousand dollars."

"Not enough."

"Okay. I can go as high as five. You get more when you return to the States."

"It sounds important."

"It could be."

"I have your word?"

He nodded.

Marion said, "I had your word once before, Indy.

Last time we met you gave me your word you'd be back. Remember that?"

"I *am* back."

"The same bastard," she said.

She was silent for a time, moving around the side of the bar until she was standing close to him. "Give me the five grand now and come back tomorrow."

"Why tomorrow?"

"Because I said so. Because it's time I started to call some shots where you're concerned."

He took out the money, gave it to her. "Okay," he said. "I trust you."

"You're an idiot."

"Yeah," he sighed. "I've heard that."

He got down from the stool. He wondered where he was going to spend the night. In a snowbank, he supposed. If Marion had her way. He turned to leave.

"Do one thing for me," she said.

He turned to look at her.

"Kiss me."

"Kiss you?"

"Yeah. Go on. Refresh my memory."

"What if I refuse?"

"Then don't come back tomorrow."

He laughed. He leaned toward her, surprised by his own eagerness, then by the sudden wildness of the kiss, by the way she pulled at his hair, the way her tongue forced itself between his lips and moved slickly against the roof of his mouth. The kiss of the child was long gone; this was different, the kiss of a woman who has learned the nature of lovemaking. She drew herself away, smiled, reached for her drink.

"Now get the hell out of my place," Marion said.

She watched him go, watched the door close behind him. She didn't move for a time; then she undid the scarf she wore around her neck. A chain hung suspended between her breasts. She pulled on the chain, at the end of which there was a sun-shaped bronze medallion with a crystal set into it.

She rubbed it thoughtfully between thumb and forefinger.

Indy trembled in the freezing night air as he went toward the car. He sat inside for a time. What was he supposed to do now? Drive around this hole until morning? He wasn't likely to find any three-star hotel in Patan, nor did he relish the idea of spending the night asleep in the car. By morning he'd be frozen solid as a Popsicle. Maybe, he thought, I'll give her some time and then she'll soften and I can go back; maybe she can show me some of that hospitality for which innkeepers are supposed to be famous. He cupped his hands and blew into them for heat, then he started the engine of the car. Even the rim of the steering wheel was chilly to touch.

Indy drove off slowly.

He didn't see the shadow in the doorway across the street, the shadow of the raincoated man who had boarded the DC-3 in Shanghai, a man by the name of Toht who had been sent to Patan at the express request of the Third Reich Special Antiquities Collection. Toht moved across the street, accompanied by his hired help—a German thug with an eyepatch, a Nepalese in a fur jacket and a Mongolian who carried a submachine gun as if anything that might move in his line of vision would automatically be a target.

They paused outside the door of The Raven, watching Indiana Jones's car depart in a flare of red taillights.

Marion stood reflectively in front of the coal fire, a poker in her hand. She stabbed at the dying flames and suddenly, despite herself, despite what she considered a weakness, she was crying. That damn Jones, she thought. Ten years down the road, down a hard bloody road, he comes dancing back into my life with more of his promises. And the ten years collapsed, time flicked away like the pages of a book, and she was remembering how it had been back then —fifteen years old and fancying herself in love with the handsome young archaeologist, the young man her father had warned her about. She remembered his saying, "You'll only get hurt, even if you'll get over it in time." Well, the hurt had been true and real—but the rest of it wasn't. Maybe it was true what they sometimes said, that old wives' tale—maybe you never really forgot the first man, the first love. Certainly she had never forgotten the delicious quality, the trembling, the feeling that she might die from the sheer anticipation of the kiss, the embrace. Nothing had touched that wicked heightening of the senses, that feeling of floating through the world as if she were insubstantial, flimsy, as if she might be transparent when held up to light.

She decided she was being stupid, crying, all because Mr. Big Shot Archaeologist comes strutting through the door. The hell with him, she said to herself. He's only good for the money now.

Confused, she went to the bar. She slipped the chain from her neck, laid the medallion on the bar. She picked up the money Indy had left and, reaching behind the bar, put it inside a small wooden box. She was still staring at the medallion, which lay in the shadow of the huge taxidermic raven, when she heard a noise at the door. She whipped quickly around to see four men come in, and at once she understood that there was trouble and that the trouble had come in the wake of good old Indiana Jones. What the hell has he landed me in? she wondered.

"We're closed. I'm sorry," she said.

The one in the raincoat, who had a face like an open razor, smiled. "We didn't come for a drink," he said. His voice was heavily accented, German.

"Oh." And she watched the razor's companions, the Nepalese and the Mongolian (dear God, he has a machine gun), poke around the place. She thought of the medallion lying on the surface of the bar. The guy with the eye patch passed very close to it.

"What do you want?" she asked.

"Precisely the same thing your friend Indiana

Jones is looking for," the German said. "I'm sure he must have mentioned it."

"No, I'm sorry."

"Ah," the man said. "Has he acquired it, then?"

"I don't think I understand you," she said.

The man sat down, drawing his raincoat up. "Forgive me for not introducing myself. Toht. Arnold Toht. Jones asked about a certain medallion, did he not?"

"He might have done . . ." She was thinking about the gun that lay on the ledge behind the stuffed raven, wondering how quickly she could reach it.

"Don't play silly games with me, please," Toht said.

"All right. He's coming back tomorrow. Why don't you come back then too, and we'll hold an auction, if you're *that* interested."

Toht shook his head. "I'm afraid not. I have to have the object tonight, Fräulein." He rose and looked in the fire, bending, lifting the poker from the embers.

Marion pretended to yawn. "I don't have it. Come back tomorrow. I'm tired."

"I am sorry you're tired. However . . ." He motioned with his head. The Mongolian caught Marion from behind, pinning her arms at her back, while Toht pulled the red-hot poker from the fire and moved toward her.

"I think I see your point," she said. "Look, I can be reasonable—"

"I'm sure, I'm sure." Toht sighed as if he were a man weary of violence, but that sound was misleading. He advanced toward her, still holding the poker close to her face. She could feel its heat against her skin. She twisted her face to the side and struggled against the grip of the Mongolian, but he was too strong.

"Wait, I'll show you where it is!"

Toht said, "You had your opportunity for that, my dear."

A sadist of the old school, she thought. The medallion doesn't matter a bit to him, only the sight of that poker searing my face. She struggled again, but it was useless. Okay, she decided, you've lost everything else, you might as well lose your looks, too. She tried to bite the big man's arm, but he simply slapped the side of her face, stinging her with an open palm that smelled of wax.

She stared at the poker.

Too close. Five inches. Four. Three.

The sickening smell of hot metal.

And then—

Then it all happened too quickly for her to follow for a moment, an abrupt series of events that occurred in a blur, like an ink drawing that has been caught in the rain. She heard a crack, a violent crack, and what she saw was the European's hand go up in the air suddenly, the poker flying across the room to the window, where it wrapped itself in the curtains and started to smolder. She felt the Mongolian release her and then she realized that Indiana Jones had come back, that he was standing in the doorway with that old bullwhip of his in one hand and a pistol in the other. Indiana Jones, just like the damn cavalry coming at the last possible moment. *What the hell kept you?* she wanted to scream. But now she wanted to move, she had to move, the room was filled with all manner of violence, the air was charged like the atmosphere of an electrical storm. She swung over the bar and reached for a bottle just as Toht fired a gun at her, but the bullets were wild and she rolled over on the floor behind the counter in a rage of shattered glass. Gunfire, deafening, loud, piercing her ears.

The Mongolian, cumbersome, leveled his submachine gun. He's aiming for Indy, she realized, directly at Indy. Something to hit him with, she thought. She reached instinctively for her barman's ax handle and struck the Mongolian across the skull as hard as she could, and he went down. But then there was somebody else in the bar, somebody who'd come crashing through the door like it was made of cardboard, and she raised her face to see somebody she recognized, a Sherpa, one of the locals, a giant of a man who could be bought by anybody for a couple of glasses of booze. He came through, a whirlwind, tackling Indy from behind, crushing him to the floor.

And then Toht was shouting, "Shoot! Shoot both of them!"

The man with the eye patch sprang to life at Toht's command. He had a pistol in his hand and it was clear he was about to follow Toht to the letter. Just as she panicked, a strange thing happened: in an unlikely conspiracy of survival, Indy and the Sherpa reached for the fallen gun simultaneously, their hands clasping it. Then they turned it against their assailant and the weapon fired, striking Eye Patch, a direct hit in the throat with a force that threw him across the room. He staggered backward until he lay propped against the bar with an expression on his face that suggested a pirate keelhauled during a drunken binge.

Then the struggle was on again, the unnatural joining of forces, the weird truce, brought to an end. The pistol had fallen away from the hands of Indy, and the Sherpa, and they were rolling over and over together as each tried to grab the elusive gun. But now Toht had a clear shot at Indiana. She picked up the submachine gun that had dropped from the Mongolian's shoulder and tried to understand how it worked—how else could it work, she thought, except by pulling the trigger! She opened fire, but the weapon kicked and jumped wildly. Her shots sizzled past Toht. Then her attention was drawn to the flames spreading from the curtains toward the rest of the bar. Nobody's going to win this one, she thought. This fire is the only thing likely to come out ahead.

From the corner of her eye she watched Toht crouch at the end of the bar as the flames were bursting all around him, searing the bar. He's seen it, she thought. He's seen the medallion. She watched his hand snake toward it, saw the expression of delight on his face, and then suddenly he was screaming as the fire-blackened medallion scorched his palm, burned its shape and design, its ancient words, deep into his flesh. He couldn't hold it. The pain was too much. He staggered toward the door, clutching his burned hand. And then Marion looked back toward Indy, who was struggling with the Sherpa. The Nepalese was circling them, trying to get a clear shot at Indy. She tapped the submachine gun, but the weapon was useless, spent. The pistol, then. The pistol behind the stuffed raven. Through flame and heat she reached for it, turned, listened to the bottles of booze explode around her like Molotov cocktails, took aim at the Nepalese. One true shot, she thought. One good and true shot.

He wouldn't keep still, the bastard.

Now smoke was blinding her, choking her.

Indy kicked the Sherpa, rolling away from him, and then the Nepalese had a clear target—Indy's skull. Now! Do it now!

She squeezed the trigger.

The Nepalese rose in the air, blown upward and back by the force of the shot. And Indy looked at her gratefully through the smoke and flame, smiling.

He grabbed his bullwhip and his hat and yelled, "Let's get the hell out of here!"

"Not without that piece you wanted."

"It's here?"

Marion kicked a burning chair aside. From overhead, in a spectacular burst of flame, a wooden beam collapsed, throwing up sparks and cinders.

"Forget it!" Indy shouted. "I want you out of here. Now!"

But Marion darted toward the place where Toht had dropped the medallion. Coughing, trying not to breathe, her eyes smarting and watering from the black smoke, she reached down and picked up the medallion in the loose scarf that hung round her neck. And then she looked for the wooden money-box.

"Unbelievable!" Ashes. Five grand up in smoke.

Indiana Jones grabbed her by the wrist, dragging her through the fire toward the door. "Let's go! Let's go!" he screamed.

They made it out into the chill night air just as the place began to crumble, as smoke and fire poured upward into the darkness in a wild display of destruction. Cinders, glowing embers, burning timbers—they danced through the fiery roof toward the moon.

From the other side of the street Indy and Marion stood and watched it.

She noticed he still had his hand around her wrist. That touch. It had been so long, so much time had dwindled away, and even as she remembered the contact, the friction of his skin upon hers, she fought the memory away. She took her arm from his hand and moved slightly away.

She stared at the bonfire again, and said nothing for a time. Timbers crackled with the sound of pigs being scorched over spits. "I figure you owe me," she said, finally, "I figure you owe me plenty."

"For starters?"

"For starters, this," and she held the medallion toward him. "I'm your partner, mister. Because this little gismo is still my property."

"Partner?" he said.

"Damn right."

They watched the fire a little longer, neither of them noticing Arnold Toht slinking away through the alleys that ran from the main street—slinking like a rat heading through a maze.

In the car Marion said, "What next?"

Indy was silent for a moment before he answered, "Egypt."

"Egypt?" Marion looked at him as the car moved through the dark. "You take me to the most exotic places."

The silhouettes of mountains appeared; a pale moon broke the night sky. Indy watched clouds disperse. He wondered why he felt a sudden apprehension, a feeling that passed when he heard Marion laugh.

"What's the joke?"

"You," she said. "You and that bullwhip."

"Don't mock it, kid. It saved your life."

"I couldn't believe it when I saw you. I'd forgotten about that ratty old whip. I remember how you used to practice with it every day. Those old bottles on the wall and you standing there with the whip." And she laughed again.

A memory, Indy thought. He recalled the odd fascination he'd had with the bullwhip ever since he'd seen a whip act in a traveling circus as a seven-year-old kid. Wide-eyed in wonder, watching the whip artist defy all logic. And then the hours of practice, a devotion that nobody, himself included, could truly explain.

"Do you ever go anywhere without it?" she asked.

"I never take it to class when I have to teach," he said.

"I bet you sleep with it, huh?"

"Now, that all depends," he said.

She was silent, staring out into the Himalayan night. Then she said, "Depends on what?"

"Work it out for yourself," Jones said.

"I think I get the picture."

He glanced at her once, then returned his eyes to the pocked road ahead.

6: The Tanis Digs, Egypt

A hot sun scorched the sand, burning on the wasteland that stretched from one horizon to the other. In such a place as this, Belloq thought, you might imagine the whole world a scalded waste, a planet without vegetation, without buildings, without people. *Without people.* Something in this thought pleased him. He had always found treachery the most common currency among human beings—consequently, he had trafficked in that currency himself. And if it wasn't treachery people understood best, then its alternative was violence. He shaded his eyes against the sun and moved forward, watching the dig that was taking place. An elaborate dig—but then, that was how the Germans liked things. Elaborate, with needless circumstance and pomp. He stuck his hands in his pockets, watching the trucks and the bulldozers, the Arab excavators, the German supervisors. And the silly Dietrich, who seemed to fancy himself overlord of all, barking orders, rushing around as if pursued by a whirlwind.

He paused, watching but not watching now, an absent look in his eyes. He was remembering the meeting with the Führer, recalling how embarrassingly fulsome the little man had been. *You are the world's expert in this matter, I understand, and I want the best.* Fulsome and ignorant. False compliments yielding to some deranged Teutonic rhetoric, the thousand-year Reich, the grandiose historic scheme that could only have been dreamed up by a lunatic. Belloq had simply stopped listening, staring at the Führer in wonderment, amazed that the destiny of any country should fall into such clumsy hands. *I want the Ark, of course. The Ark belongs in the Reich. Something of such antiquity belongs in Germany.*

Belloq closed his eyes against the harsh sun. He tuned out the noises of the excavations, the shouts of the Germans, the occasional sounds of the Arabs. The Ark, he thought. It doesn't belong to any one man, any one place, any single time. But its secrets are mine, if there are secrets to be had. He opened his eyes again and stared at the dig, the huge craters hacked out of sand, and he felt a certain vibration, a positive intuition, that the great prize was somewhere nearby. He could feel it, sense its power, he could hear the whisper of the thing that would soon become a roar. He took his hands from his pockets and stared at the medallion that lay in the center of his palm. And what he understood as he stared at it was a curious obsession—and a fear that he might yield to it in the end. You lust after a thing long enough, as he had lusted after the Ark, and you start to feel the edge of some madness that is almost . . . almost what?

Divine.

Maybe it was the madness of the saints and the zealots.

A sense of a vision so awesome that all reality simply faded.

An awareness of a power so inexpressible, so cosmic, that the thin fabric of what you assumed to be the real world parted, disintegrated, and you were left with an understanding that, like God's, surpassed all things.

Perhaps. He smiled to himself.

He moved around the edge of the excavations, skirting past the trucks and the bulldozers. He clutched the medallion tight in his hand. And then he thought about how those thugs dispatched by Dietrich to Nepal had botched the whole business. He experienced disgust.

Those morons, though, had brought back something which served his purposes.

It was the whimpering Toht who had shown Belloq his palm, asking for sympathy, Belloq supposed. Not realizing he had, seared into his flesh, a perfect copy of the very thing he had failed to retrieve.

It had been amusing to see Toht sitting restlessly for hours, days, while he, Belloq, painstakingly fashioned a perfect copy. He'd worked meticulously, trying to recreate the original. But it wasn't the real thing, the *historic* thing. It was accurate enough for his calculations concerning the map room and the Well of the Souls, but he had wanted the original badly.

Belloq put the medallion back inside his pocket and walked over to where Dietrich was standing. For a long time he said nothing, pleased by the feeling that his presence gave the German some discomfort. Eventually Dietrich said, "It's going well, don't you think?"

Belloq nodded, shielding his eyes again. He was thinking of something else now, something that disturbed him. It was the piece of information that had been brought back, by one of Dietrich's lackeys, from Nepal. *Indiana Jones.*

Of course, he should have known that Jones would appear on the scene sooner or later. Jones was troublesome, even if the rivalry between them always ended in his defeat. He didn't have, Belloq thought, the cunning. The instinct. The killing edge.

But now he had been seen in Cairo with the girl who was Ravenwood's daughter.

Dietrich turned to him and said, "Have you come to a decision about that other matter we discussed?"

"I think so," Belloq said.

"I assume it is the decision I imagined you would reach?"

"Assumptions are often arrogant, my friend."

Dietrich looked at the other man silently.

Belloq smiled. "In this case, though, you are probably correct."

"You wish me to attend to it?"

Belloq nodded. "I trust I can leave the details to you."

"Naturally," Dietrich said.

7: Cairo

The dark was warm and still, the air like a vacuum. It was dry, hard to breathe, as if all moisture had evaporated in the heat of the day. Indy sat with Marion in a coffeehouse, rarely taking his eyes from the door. For hours now, they had been moving through back streets and alleys, staying away from the central thoroughfares—and yet he'd had the feeling all the time that he was being watched. Marion looked exhausted, drained, her long hair damp from sweat. And it was clear to Indy that she was becoming more and more impatient with him: now she was staring at him over the rim of her coffee cup in an accusing fashion. He watched the door, scrutinized the patrons that came and went, and sometimes turned his face upward to catch the thin passage of air that blew from the creaking overhead fan.

"You might have the decency to tell me how long we're going to creep around like this," Marion said.

"Is that what we're doing?"

"It would be obvious to a blind man that we're hiding from something, Jones. And I'm beginning to wonder why I left Nepal. I had a thriving business, don't forget. A business you torched."

He looked at her and smiled and thought how vibrant she appeared when she was on the edge of anger. He reached across the small table and touched the back of her hand. "We're hiding from the kind of jokers we encountered in Nepal."

"Okay. I buy that. But for how long?"

"Until I get the feeling that it's safe to go."

"Safe to go where? What do you have in mind?"

"I'm not exactly without friends."

She sighed and finished her coffee, then leaned back in her chair and shut her eyes. "Wake me when you've made up your mind, okay?"

Indy stood up and pulled her to her feet. "It's time," he said. "We can leave now."

"Brother," she said. "Just as I was trying to get some beauty sleep."

They went out into the alleyway, which was almost deserted.

Indy paused, looking this way and that. Then he took her by the hand and began to walk.

"You want to give me some idea of where we're headed exactly?"

"The house of Sallah."

"And who is Sallah?"

"The best digger in Egypt."

He only hoped Sallah still lived in the same place. And beyond that there was another hope, a deeper one, that Sallah was employed in the Tanis dig.

He paused at a corner, a junction where two narrow alleys branched away from one another. "This way," he said, still pulling at Marion's arm.

She sighed, then yawned. She followed.

Something moved in the shadows behind them, something that might have been human. It moved without noise, gliding quickly over the concrete; it knew only to follow the two people who walked ahead of it.

Indy was welcomed into Sallah's house as if only a matter of weeks had passed since they last met. But it had been years. Even so, Sallah had changed very little. The same intelligent eyes in the brown face, the same energetic cheerfulness, the hospitable warmth. They embraced as Sallah's wife, a large woman called Fayah, ushered them inside the house.

The warmth of the greeting touched Indy. The comfortable quality of the house made him feel at ease immediately, too. When they sat down at the table in the dining room, eating food that Fayah had produced with all the haste of a culinary miracle, he looked over at the other table in the corner, where Sallah's children sat.

"Some things change after all," he said. He placed a small cube of lamb into his mouth and nodded his head in the direction of the kids.

"Ah," Sallah said. His wife smiled in a proud way. "The last time there were not so many."

"I can remember only three," Indy said.

"Now there are nine," Sallah said.

"Nine," and Indy shook his head in wonderment.

Marion got up from the table and went over to where the children sat. She talked to each of them, touched them, played briefly with them, and then she came back. Indy imagined he saw some kind of look, something indeterminate yet obviously connected with a love of children, pass between Marion and Fayah. For his part he'd never had time for kids in his life; they constituted the kind of clutter he didn't need.

"We have made a decision to stop at nine," Sallah said.

"I'd call that wise," Indy said.

Sallah reached for a date, chewed on it silently for a moment and then said, "It really is good to see you again, Indiana. I've thought about you often. I even intended to write, but I'm a bad correspondent. And I assumed you were even worse."

"You assumed right." Indy reached for a date himself. It was plump and delicious.

Sallah was smiling. "I won't ask you immediately, but I imagine you haven't come all the way to Cairo just to see me. Am I correct?"

"Correct."

Sallah looked suddenly knowing, suddenly sly. "In fact, I would even place a bet on your reason for being here."

Indy stared at his old friend, smiled, said nothing.

Sallah said, "Of course, I am not a gambling man."

"Of course," Indy said.

"We don't talk business at the table," Fayah remarked, looking imposing.

"Later," Indy said. He glanced at Marion, who appeared half-asleep now.

"Later, when everything is quiet," Sallah said.

There was a silence in the room for a second, and then suddenly the place was filled with noise, as if something had erupted at the table where the kids sat.

Fayah turned and tried to silence the pandemonium. But the kids weren't listening to her voice, because they were busy with something else. She rose, saying, "We have guests. You forget your manners."

But they still didn't hear her. It was only when she approached their table that they became silent, revealing in their midst a small monkey sitting upright in the center of the table, chewing on a piece of bread.

Fayah said, "Who brought this animal in here? Who did it?"

The children didn't answer. They were busy laughing at the antics of the creature, which strutted around with the bread in its paws. It bounced over, performed a perfect handstand and then leaped from the table and skipped across the floor to Marion. It jumped up into her lap and kissed her quickly on the cheek. She laughed.

"A kissing monkey, huh?" she said. "I like you too."

Fayah said, "How did it get here?"

For a time none of the children spoke. And then the one that Indy recognized as being the oldest said, "We don't know. It just appeared."

Fayah regarded her brood with disbelief. Marion said, "If you don't want to have the animal around—"

Fayah interrupted. "If you like it, Marion, then it's welcome in our home. As you are."

Marion held the monkey a moment longer before she set it down. It regarded her in a baleful way and immediately bounced back into her lap.

"It must love you," Indy said. He found animals only slightly more bothersome than children, and not quite so cute.

She put her arms around the small creature and hugged it. As he watched this behavior, Indy wondered, Who could hug a monkey that way? He turned his face toward Sallah, who was rising from the table now.

"We can go out into the courtyard," Sallah said.

Indy followed him through the door. There was trapped heat in the walled courtyard; at once he began to feel lethargic, but he knew he had to fight the tiredness a little longer.

Sallah indicated a raffia chair and Indy sat down.

"You want to talk about Tanis," Sallah said.

"You got it."

"I assumed so," Sallah said.

"Then you're working there?"

Sallah was quiet, looking up into the night sky for a time.

"Indy," he said. "This afternoon I personally broke through into the Map Room at Tanis."

This news, though he had somehow expected it, nevertheless shook him. For a time his mind was empty, thoughtless, as if all perceptions, all memories, had fled into some dark void. *The Map Room at Tanis.* And he thought of Abner Ravenwood after a while, of a lifetime spent searching for the Ark, of dying in madness because the Ark had possessed him. Then he considered himself and the strange jealous reaction he had begun to experience, almost as if *he* should have been the first to break through into the Map Room, as if it were *his* right, like a legacy Ravenwood had passed down to him in some obscure way. Irrational thinking, he told himself.

He looked at Sallah and said, "They're moving fast."

"The Nazis are well organized, Indy."

"Yeah. At least they're good at something, even if it's only following orders."

"Besides, they have the Frenchman in charge."

"The Frenchman?"

"Belloq."

Indy was silent, sitting upright in his chair. *Belloq.* Wasn't there anywhere in the world the bastard wouldn't turn up? He felt angry at first, and after that something else, a feeling he began to enjoy slowly, a sense of competition, the quiet thrill of seeing the opportunity to get even. He smiled for the first time. *Belloq, I'll get you this time,* he thought. And there was a hard determination in the prospect.

He took the medallion from his pocket and passed it to Sallah.

"They might have discovered the Map Room," he said. "But they won't get very far without *this,* will they?"

"I take it this is the headpiece of the Staff of Ra?"

"That's right. The markings on it are unfamiliar to me. What do you make of it?"

Sallah shook his head. "Personally, nothing. But I know someone who would. I can take you to meet him tomorrow."

"I'd appreciate that," Indy said. He took the medallion back from Sallah and put it in his pocket. Safe, he thought. Without this, Belloq might just as well be blind. A fine sense of triumph there, he told himself. *René, this one is all mine.* If I can arrange some way to get around the Nazis.

He asked, "How many Germans are involved in the dig?"

"A hundred or so," Sallah said. "They are also very well equipped."

"I thought so." Indy closed his eyes and sat back. He could feel sleep press in on him. I'll think of something, he said to himself. Soon.

"It worries me, Indy," Sallah said.

"What does?"

"The Ark. If it is there at Tanis . . ." Sallah lapsed into silence, an expression of suppressed anguish on his face. "It is not something man was meant to disturb. Death has always surrounded it. Always. It is not of this world, if you understand what I mean."

"I understand," Indy said.

"And the Frenchman . . . he's clearly obsessed with the thing. I look in his eyes and I see something I cannot describe. The Germans don't like him. He doesn't care. He doesn't even seem to notice anything. The Ark, that's all he ever thinks about. And the way he watches everything—he misses nothing. When he entered the Map Room . . . how can I describe his face? He was transported into a place where I would have no desire to go myself."

Out of nowhere, shaken out of the hot dark, there was an abrupt wind that blew grit and sand—a wind that died as sharply as it had risen.

"You must sleep now," Sallah said. "My house is yours, of course."

"And I'm grateful."

Both men went indoors; the house was quiet.

Indy walked past the room where Marion was sleeping; he paused outside the closed door, listening to the faint sound of her breathing. A child's breathing, he thought—and he had a flash of Marion years ago, when their affair, if that was the word, had taken place. But the desire he felt right then was a different thing altogether: it was a desire for the woman now.

He was pleased with the feeling.

He passed along the corridor, followed by Sallah.

The child is buried, he thought; only the woman lives now.

Sallah asked, "You resist temptation, Indy?"

"Didn't you know about my puritan streak?"

Sallah shrugged, smiled in a mysterious way, as Indy closed the door of the guest room and went toward the bed. He heard Sallah move along the corridor, then the house was silent. He closed his eyes, expecting sleep to come in quickly—but it didn't. It remained an elusive shadow just beyond the range of his mind.

He turned around restlessly. Why couldn't he just let go and sleep? *You resist temptation, Indy?* He pressed his knuckles against his eyelids: he turned around some more, but what he kept seeing inside his head was a picture of Marion sleeping quietly in her room. He got out of bed and opened the door. Go back to bed, Indy, he said to himself. You don't know what you're doing.

He stepped out into the corridor and walked slowly —a burglar on tiptoe, he thought—toward Marion's room. Outside her door he paused. Turn around. Go back to your insomnia. He twisted the handle, entered the room and saw her lying on top of the bed covers. Moonlight flooded the room like a silver reflection thrown by the wings of a vast night moth. She didn't move. She lay with her face to one side, arms across her stomach; the light made soft shadows around her mouth. Go back, he thought. Get back now.

Beautiful. She looked so beautiful, vulnerable, there. A sleeping woman and the touch of the moon—a dizzying combination. He found himself going toward the bed, then sitting on the edge of the mattress. He stared at her face, raised his hand, placed the tips of his fingers lightly against one cheek. Almost at once she opened her eyes.

She said nothing for a time. Her eyes seemed black in the room. He put a finger over her lips.

"You want to know why I'm sitting here, right?" he asked.

"I can hardly begin to guess," she said. "You've come to explain the intricacies of Mr. Roosevelt's New Deal? Or maybe you expect me to swoon in the moonlight."

"I don't expect anything."

She laughed. "Everybody expects something. It's a little lesson I picked up along the way."

He lifted her hand, felt it tremble a little.

She didn't say anything as he lowered his face and

kissed her on the mouth. The kiss he received in return was quick and hard and without emotion. He drew his face away and looked at her for a time. She sat up, drawing a bedsheet over herself. The nightdress was transparent and her breasts were visible—firm breasts, not those of a child now.

"I'd like you to leave," she said.

"Why?"

"I don't have to give reasons."

Indy sighed. "Do you really hate me that much?"

She stared at the window. "Nice moon," she said.

"I asked you a question."

"You can't just trample your way back into my life, Indy. You can't just kick over all the props I've made for myself and expect me to pick up the pieces of the past. Don't you see that?"

"Yeah," he said.

"That's my lecture. Now I need some sleep. So go."

He got up slowly.

When he reached the door he heard her say, "I want you too. Don't you think I do? Give it some time, okay? Let's see what happens."

"Sure," and then he stepped out into the corridor, unable to silence the echo of disappointment that seemed to roll inside his head. He stood in the moonlight that came in slivers through the window at the end of the hallway, and he wondered—as his desire began to fade—whether he'd made an ass of himself. It wouldn't be for the first time, he thought.

She couldn't sleep after he'd gone. She sat by the window and stared at the skyline of the city, the domes, minarets, flat roofs. Why did he have to try this soon, anyhow? The damned man had never learned patience, had he? He was as reckless in matters of the heart as he was in everything else. He didn't understand that people needed time; it might not be the great healer, but it was a lot better than iodine. She couldn't just haul herself out of the past and land, like some alien creature from a far galaxy, in the rude awakening of Indiana Jones's present. It had to be mapped more gently.

If there was anything to be taken; if there was anything to be mapped.

The figure moved quickly through the cloakroom where Indy and Marion had left their suitcases and belongings. It moved with unnatural stealth, opening cases, sifting through clothes, picking up pieces of paper, examining them with laborious slowness. It did not find what it had been trained to discover. It understood it had to look for a particular shape—a drawing, an object, it didn't matter as long as it had the shape. When it found nothing, it understood its owner would be disappointed. And that would mean a lack of food. That might even mean punishment. It made a picture of the shape once more in its brain: the shape of the sun, small marks around it, a hole in the center. It began to rummage again.

Again, it found nothing.

The monkey skipped lightly into the corridor, removed some items of food scraps from the table where it had played before with the pretty woman, then swung out through an open window and into the dark.

8: Cairo

The afternoon was sunny, the sky almost a pure white. Whiteness reflected from everything, from walls, clothing, glass, as if the light had become a frost that lay across all surfaces.

"Did we need the monkey?" Indy asked. They were going quickly through the crowded street, passing the bazaars, the merchants.

'It followed me, I didn't exactly *bring* it," Marion said.

"It must be attached to you."

"It's not so much *me* it's attached to, Indy. It thinks you're its father, see? It's got some of your looks, anyhow."

"My looks, your brains."

Marion was silent for a while before asking, "Why haven't you found yourself a nice girl to settle down with and raise nine kids?"

"Who says I haven't?"

She glanced at him. It pleased him to think he saw a brief flash of panic on her face, of envy. "You couldn't take the responsibility. My dad really had you figured, Indy. He said you were a bum."

"He was being generous."

"The most gifted bum he ever trained, but a bum

anyhow. He loved you, you know that? It took a hell of a lot for you to alienate him."

Indy sighed. "I don't want to rehash it, Marion."

"I don't want that, either," she said. "But sometimes I like to remind you."

"An emotional hypodermic, is that it?"

"A jag, right. You need it to keep you in your place."

Indy began to walk more quickly. There were times when, despite his own defenses, she managed to slide just under his skin. It was like the unexpected desire he'd felt last night. I don't need it, he thought. I don't need it in my life. Love means some kind of order, and you don't want order when you've become accustomed to thriving on chaos.

"You haven't told me where we're going yet," Marion said.

"We meet Sallah, then we go see Sallah's expert, Imam."

"What I like is how you drag me everywhere," Marion said. "It reminds me of my father sometimes. He dragged me around the globe like I was a rag."

They reached a fork in the street. All at once the monkey pulled itself free of Marion's hand and ran through the crowd in quick, loping movements.

"Hey!" Marion shouted. "Get back here!"

Indy said, relieved, "Let it go."

"I was just getting used to it."

Indy gave her a dirty look, caught her by the hand and made her keep up with him.

The monkey scuttled along, slipping through the crowds that jammed the street. It avoided the outstretched hands of people who wanted to touch it, then it turned a corner and stepped into a doorway. There it leaped into the arms of the man who had trained it. He had trained it very well. He held it against his body, popped a confection in its mouth and then moved out of the doorway. The monkey was better than a bloodhound, and a hundred times smarter.

The man looked along the narrow street, raising his face toward the rooftops. He waved.

From a nearby rooftop somebody waved back.

Then he patted the animal. It had done its job very well, following the two who were to be killed, tracking them as diligently as a predator but with infinitely more charm than that.

Good, the man thought. Very good.

Indy and Marion turned into a small square, a place cramped by the stalls of vendors, the crowds of shoppers. Indy stopped suddenly. That old instinct was working on him now, working over his nerve ends, making him tingle. *Something is about to happen,* he thought.

He looked through the crowds. Exactly what?

"Why have we stopped?" Marion asked.

Indy said nothing.

This crowd. How could he tell anything from this bunch of people? He reached inside his jacket and gripped the handle of the bullwhip. He stared into the crowd again. There was a group that moved toward him, moved with more purpose than any of the ordinary shoppers.

A few Arabs. A couple of guys who were European.

With his sharp eyesight, Indy saw the flash of something metallic and he thought, *A dagger*. He saw it glint in the hand of an Arab who was approaching them quickly. Indy hauled the whip out, lashed, listened as it split air with the sound of some menacing melody; it curled around the hand of the Arab and the dagger went slicing harmlessly into nowhere. But then there were more people advancing toward them and he had to think fast.

"Get out of here," he said to Marion, and gave her a quick shove. "Run!"

But Marion wasn't running. Instead, she seized a broom from a nearby stall and swung it into the throat of another Arab, who slumped to the ground.

"Go," Indy said again. "Go!"

"The hell I will," she said.

There were too many of them, Indy thought. Too many to fight, even with her help. He watched the blade of an ax swing, and he struck with the whip again, this time around the Arab's neck. He pulled tight and the man moaned before he dropped. And then one of the Europeans was on him, trying to drag the whip from his hand. Indy swung his leg high, smashing his foot into the man's body. The man clutched his chest and fell backward into a fruit stall, toppling amid spilled and squashed vegetables that looked like a mad still life. Indy noticed a gate in a wall and reached for Marion, pushing her through it, then drawing the bolt so she couldn't get out despite her cries and protestations. He looked around the square, striking with his whip, knocking away the props of stalls. Chaos, utter chaos, and he loved it. A blade swung at him and he ducked just in time, hearing the steel whistle above his head. Then he flicked his whip and wrapped it around the Arab's ankles, bringing him down in a pile of scattered vases and broken jars, while the merchant screamed angrily.

He surveyed the wreckage. He wondered if there were any more takers. The urge for action he felt was exalting.

Nobody moved except the merchants who had seen their stalls wrecked by some lunatic with a bullwhip. He began to back away, moving toward the door in the wall, reaching for the bolt as he did so. He could hear Marion banging on the wood. But before he could slide the bolt, a burnoosed figure lunged toward him with a machete. Indy raised his arm to fend off the blow, catching the man by the wrist and struggling with him.

Marion stopped banging and backed away from the door, looking for some other access to the square. Damn Indy, she thought, for thinking he's got some God-given right to protect me! Damn him for an attitude that belongs to the Middle Ages! She turned down the narrow alleyway in which she found herself and then stopped dead: an Arab was walking toward her, walking in quick, menacing steps. She slipped down the nearest alley, heard the man coming up from behind.

A dead end.

A wall.

She hoisted herself onto the top of the wall, listening to the Arab grunt as he chased her. She scrambled over, got to the other side, hid herself in an alcove between buildings. The Arab unsuspectingly went past her and, after a moment, Marion peered out. He was coming back again, this time in the company of one of the Europeans. She stepped back inside the alcove, breathing hard even as she tried despairingly to still her lungs, to stop the rattle of her heart. What do you do in a situation like this? she thought. You hide, don't you? You plain hide. She had stepped back further into the alcove, seeking the shadows, the dark places, when she encountered a rattan basket. Okay, she thought, so you feel like one of the Forty Thieves, but there was an old saying about any port in a storm, right? She climbed inside the basket, pulled the lid in place and remained there in a crouching position. Be still. Don't move. She could hear, through the slits in the rattan, the sound of the two men skulking around. They spoke to one another in an English so broken, she thought, as to be in need of a major splint.

Look here.

In this place I already looked.

She remained very still.

What she didn't see, what she couldn't see, was the monkey sitting on a wall that overlooked the alcove; she could hear it chattering suddenly, wildly, and it was a few moments before she understood what the noise was. That monkey, she thought. It followed me. The affectionate betrayal. Please, monkey, go away, leave me alone. But she felt herself being raised up now, the basket lifted. She peered through the narrow slats of the basket and saw that the Arab and the European were her bearers, that she was being carted, like refuse, on their shoulders. She struggled. She hammered with her fists against the lid, which was tight now.

In the bazaar Indy had pushed the man with the machete aside; but the place was in turmoil now, angry Arab merchants milling around, gesticulating wildly at the crazy man with the whip. Indy backed away against the door, fumbled for the bolt, saw the machete come toward him again. This time he lunged with his foot, knocking the man backward into the rest of the crowd. Then he worked the door open and was out in the alley, looking this way and that for some sign of her. Nothing. Only two guys at the other end of the alley carrying a basket.

Where the hell did she go?

And then, as if from nowhere, he heard her voice call his name, and the echo was strangely chilling.

The basket.

He saw the lid move as the two carriers turned the corner. Briefly, a strange chattering sound drew his attention from the basket, and he looked upward to see the monkey perched on the wall. It might have been deriding him. He was filled with an overwhelming urge to draw his pistol and murder the thing with one well-placed shot. Instead, he ran quickly in the direction of the two men. He took the same turn they had made, seeing how fast they were running ahead of him with the basket wobbling between them.

How could those guys move so quickly while they carried Marion's weight? he wondered. They were always one turn ahead of him, always one step in front. He followed them along busy thoroughfares filled with shoppers and merchants, where he had to push his way through frantically. He couldn't lose sight of that basket, he couldn't let it slip away like this. He pushed and shoved, he thrust people aside, he ignored their complaints and outcries. Keep moving. Don't lose sight of her.

And then he was conscious of a weird noise, a chanting sound that had somber undertones, a certain melancholy to it. He couldn't place it, but somehow it stopped him; he was disoriented. When he started to move again, he realized he had lost her. He couldn't see the basket now.

He started to run again, pushing through the crowd. And the strange sound of the lament, if that was what it was, became louder, more piercing.

At the corner of an alley he stopped.

There were two Arabs in front of him carrying a rattan basket.

Immediately, he drew his whip and brought one of them down, hauled the whip away, then let it flash again. It cracked against the other Arab's leg, encircling it, entwining it like a slender reptile. The basket toppled over and he stepped toward it.

No Marion.

Confused, he looked at what had spilled out of the thing.

Guns, rifles, ammo.

The wrong basket!

He backed out of the alley and continued up the main street of bazaars, and the odd wailing sound became louder still.

He entered a large square, overwhelmed by the sudden sight of misery all around him: a square of beggars, the limbless, the blind, the half-born who held out stumps of arms in front of themselves in some mindless groping for help. There was the smell of sweat and urine and excrement here, a pungency that filled the air with the tangibility of a solid object.

He crossed the square, avoiding the beggars.

And then he had to stop.

Now he knew the nature of the moaning sound.

At the far side of the square there was a funeral procession moving. Large and long, obviously the funeral march of some prominent citizen. Riderless horses hauled the coffin, priests chanted from the Koran, keening women walked up front with their heads wrapped in scarves, servants moved behind, and at the rear, cumbersome and clumsy, came the sacrificial buffalo.

He stared at the procession for a time. How the hell could he go through that line?

He looked at the coffin, ornate, opulent, held aloft; and then he noticed, through a brief break in the line, the basket being carried by the two men toward a canvas-covered truck parked in the farthest corner of the square. It was impossible to be sure over the noise of the mourners, but he thought he heard Marion screaming from inside.

He was about to move forward and shove his way through the procession when it happened.

From the truck a machine gun opened fire, raking the square, scattering the line of mourners and the mob of beggars. The priests kept up their chant until the blasts burst through the coffin itself, sending splinters of wood flying, causing the mummified corpse to slide through the broken lid to the ground. The mourners wailed with renewed interest. Indy zigzagged toward a well on the far side of the square, squeezing off a couple of shots in the direction of the truck. He slid behind the well, popping up in time to see the rattan basket being thrown into the back of the truck. Just then, almost out of his line of vision, barely noticeable, a black sedan pulled away. The truck, too, began to move.

It swung out of the square.

Before it could go beyond his sight, Indy took careful aim, an aim more precise than any other in his lifetime, and squeezed the trigger. The driver of the truck slumped forward against the wheel. The truck swerved, hit a wall, rolled over.

As he was about to move toward it, he stopped in horror.

He realized then he could never feel anything so intense in his life again, never so much pain, so much anguish, such a terrible, heavy sense of numbness.

He realized all this as he watched the truck explode, flames bursting from it, fragments flying, the whole thing wrecked; and what he also realized was that the basket had been thrown into the back of an ammunitions truck.

That Marion was dead.

Killed by a bullet from his own gun.

How could it be?

He shut his eyes, hearing nothing now, conscious only of the white sun beating against his closed lids.

He walked for what seemed like a long time, unknowing, uncaring, his mind drifting back time and again to that point where he had leveled the gun and shot the driver. Why? Why hadn't he considered the possibility that the truck might be carrying something dangerous?

You ruined her life when she was a girl.

Now you've ended it when she was a woman.

He walked the narrow streets, the alleys thronged with people, and he blamed himself over and over for the death of Marion.

It was more pain than he could think about, more than he could bear. And he knew of only one remedy. He knew of only one reliable form of self-medication. So he found himself walking toward the bar where, earlier, he had arranged to meet Sallah. That seemed locked in some dim past now, another world, a different life.

Even a different man.

He saw the bar, a rundown place. He stepped inside and was assailed by thick tobacco smoke, the smell of spilled booze. He sat on a stool by the bar. He ordered a fifth of bourbon and drank one monotonous glass after another, wondering—as he grew more inebriated—what it was that made some people tick while others were as animated as broken clocks; what was that clockwork so necessary to successful relationships that some people had and others didn't. He let the question go around in his mind until it shed its sense, floating through alcoholic perceptions like a ghost ship.

He reached for another drink. Something touched his arm and he twisted his head slowly to see the monkey on the bar. That stupid primate to which Marion had become so witlessly attached. Then he remembered that this idiot creature had splashed a kiss on Marion's cheek. Okay, Marion liked you, I can tolerate you.

"Want a drink, you baboon?"

The monkey put its head to one side, watching him.

Indy was aware of the barman watching him as if he were a fugitive from a nearby asylum. And then he was aware of something else, too: three men, Europeans—Germans, he assumed, from their accents—had crowded around him.

"Someone wishes your company," one of them said.

"I'm drinking with my friend here," Indy said.

The monkey moved slightly.

"Your company is not requested, Mr. Jones. It is *demanded.*"

He was hauled from the stool and rushed into a back room. Chattering, squealing, the monkey followed. The room was dim and his eyes smarted from smoke.

Someone was sitting at a table in the far corner.

Indy realized that this confrontation had been inevitable.

René Belloq was drinking a glass of wine and swinging a chain on which hung a watch.

"A monkey," Belloq said. "You still have admirable taste in friends, I see."

"You're a barrel of laughs, Belloq."

The Frenchman grimaced. "Your sense of repartee dismays me. It did so even when we were students, Indiana. It lacks panache."

"I ought to kill you right now—"

"Ah, I understand your urge. But I should remind you that I did not bring Miss Ravenwood into this somewhat sordid affair. And what is eating you, my old friend, is the knowledge that *you* are responsible for that. No?"

Indy sat down, slumping into the chair opposite Belloq.

Belloq leaned forward. "It also irks you that I can see through you, Jones. But the plain fact is, we are somewhat alike."

Through blood-shot eyes Indy stared at Belloq. "No need to get nasty."

"Consider this," Belloq said. "Archaelogy has always been our religion, our faith. We have both strayed somewhat from the so-called true path, admittedly. We are both given to the occasional . . . dubious . . . transaction. Our methods are not so different as you pretend. I am, if you like, a shadowy reflection of yourself. What would it take to make you the same as me, Professor? Mmm? A slight cutting edge? A sharpening of the killer instinct, yes?"

Indy said nothing. Belloq's words came to him like noises muffled by a fog. He was talking nonsense, pure nonsense, which sounded grand and true because it was delivered in a French accent that might be described as quaint, charming. What Indy heard was the hissing of some hidden snake.

"You doubt me, Jones? Consider: What brings you here? The lust for the Ark, am I correct? The old dream of antiquity. The historic relic, the quest—why, it might be a virus in your blood. You dream of things past." Belloq was smiling, swinging a watch on a chain. He said, "Look at this watch. Cheap. Nothing. Take it out into the desert and bury it for a thousand years and it becomes priceless. Men will kill for it. Men like you and me, Jones. The Ark, I admit, is different. It is a little removed from the profit motive, of course. We understand this, you and I. But the greed is still in the heart, my friend. The vice we have in common."

The Frenchman stopped smiling. There was a glassy look in his eyes, a distance, a privacy. He might have been conducting a conversation with himself. "You understand what the Ark is? It is like a transmitter. Like a radio through which one might communicate with God. And I am very close to it. Very close to it, indeed. I have waited years to be this close. And what I am talking about is beyond profit, beyond the lust of simple acquisition. I am talking about communicating with that which is contained in the Ark."

"You buy it, Belloq? You buy the mysticism? The power?"

Belloq looked disgusted. He sat back. He placed the tips of his fingers together. "Don't you?"

Indy shrugged.

"Ah, you are not sure, are you? Even you, you are not sure." Belloq lowered his voice. "I am more than sure, Jones. I am *positive.* I don't doubt it for a moment now. My researches have always led me in this direction. I *know.*"

"You're out of your mind," Indy said.

"A pity it ends this way," Belloq said. "You have at times stimulated me, a rare thing in a world so weary as this one."

"That thought makes me happy, Belloq."

"I'm glad. Truly. But everything comes to an end."

"Not a very private place for murder."

"It hardly matters. These Arabs will not interfere in a white man's business. They do not care if we kill each other off."

Belloq rose, smiling. He nodded his head in a curt way.

Indy, stalling for time, for anything, said, "I hope you learn something from your little parley with God, Belloq."

"Naturally."

Indy braced himself. There wasn't time to turn swiftly and try for his pistol, and even less time to reach his bullwhip. His assassins sat directly behind him.

Belloq was looking at his watch. "Who knows, Jones? Perhaps there will be the kind of hereafter where souls like you and me meet again. It amuses me to think that I will outwit you there as well."

There was a sound from outside now. It was an incongruous sound, the collective chattering of excited young children, a happy sound Indy associated with a Christmas morning. It wasn't what he expected to hear in the death chamber.

Belloq looked toward the door in surprise. Sallah's children, all nine of them, were trooping into the room and calling Indy's name. Indy stared as they surrounded him, as the smaller ones clambered on his knees while the others made a circle in the manner of frail human shields. Some of them began to climb on his shoulders. One had managed to drape himself over Indy's neck in a piggyback-ride style, and still another was hugging his ankles.

Belloq was frowning. "You imagine you can back out of here, do you? You imagine this insignificant human bracelet will protect you?"

"I don't imagine anything," Indy said.

"How utterly typical," Belloq answered.

They were pulling him toward the door now, he was being tugged and yanked even as they were shielding him. Sallah! It must have been Sallah's plan to risk his children and send them into this bar and contrive to get him safely out somehow. How could Sallah have taken such a risk?

Belloq was sitting once again, arms folded. The look on his face was that of a reluctant parent at a school play. He shook his head from side to side. "I will regale the next meeting of the International Archaelogical Society with the tale of your disregard for the laws governing child labor, Jones."

"You're not even a member."

Belloq smiled, but only briefly. He continued to stare at the children and then, as if he were deciding something, turned toward his accomplices. He raised his hand, a gesture that indicated they should put their weapons away.

"I have a soft spot for dogs and children, Jones. You may express your gratitude in some simple form, which would suit you. But small children will not become your saviors when we next meet."

Indy was moving back rapidly. And then he slipped out, with the kids clutching him like a precious toy. Sallah's truck was parked outside—a sight that filled Indy with delight, the first event of the day that even remotely lifted his spirits.

Belloq finished his glass of wine. He heard the truck pull away. As the sound died in the distance he thought, with an insight that surprised him vaguely, that he was not yet ready to kill Indy. That the time was not exactly ripe. It hadn't been the presence of the children at all—they hardly mattered. It was rather the fact that he wanted, somewhere in a place he did not quite fathom, a remote corner of understanding, to spare Jones, to let the man live a little longer.

There are some things, after all, worse than death, he thought.

And it amused him to ponder the agony, the anguish, that Jones would be going through: there was the girl, for one thing—which would have been punishment enough, torture enough. But there was also the fact, just as punishing, perhaps even more so, that Jones would live to see the Ark slip through his fingers.

Belloq threw back his head and laughed; and his German accomplices, their appetite for killing unsatisfied, stared at him in bewilderment.

In the truck Indy said, "Your kids have a sense of timing that would outdo the U.S. Marines, Sallah."

"I understood the situation. I had to act quickly," Sallah said.

Indy stared at the road ahead: darkness, thin lights, people parting from the path of the truck. The kids were in the back, singing and laughing. Innocent sounds, Indy thought, remembering what he wanted to forget.

"Marion . . ."

"I know," Sallah said. "The news reached me earlier. I'm sad. More than sad. What can I say to console you? How can I help your grief?"

"Nothing helps the grief, Sallah."

Sallah nodded. "I understand, of course."

"But you can help me in other ways. You can help me beat those bastards."

"You have my help, Indiana," Sallah said. "Any time at all."

Sallah was silent for a moment, driving the last stretch to his house.

"I have much news for you," he said after a while. "Some isn't good news. But it concerns the Ark."

"Hit me with it," Indy said.

"Soon. When we reach my house. And later, if you wish, we can visit the house of Imam, who will explain the markings to you."

Indy lapsed into a weary silence. He had a hangover already beginning, a violent throb in the center of his skull. And, if his senses had been sharper, his intuition less blunted by booze, he might have noticed the motorcycle that had followed the truck from the bar. But even if he had, he would not have known the rider, a man who specialized in training monkeys.

When the children had been sent indoors, Indy and Sallah went out into the walled courtyard. Sallah walked around the yard for a time before he paused by the wall and said, "Belloq has the medallion."

"What?" Immediately Indy felt inside his pocket and his fingers touched the headpiece. "You're wrong."

"He has a copy, a headpiece like yours, a crystal at the center. And there are the same markings on the piece as on the one you have."

"I can't understand it," Indy said, appalled. "I always believed there were no pictures anywhere. No duplicates. I don't get it."

Sallah said, "There's something else, Indiana."

"I'm listening."

"This morning Belloq went inside the map room. When he came out he gave us instructions about where we were to dig. A new spot, away from the general dig."

"The Well of the Souls," Indy said, in a resigned way.

"I imagine so, if he made the calculations in the Map Room."

Indy began beating the palms of his hands together. He turned once again to Sallah, taking the medallion from his pocket. "Are you sure it looked like this?"

"I saw it."

"Look again, Sallah."

The Egyptian shrugged and took the headpiece and stared at it for a time, turning it over in his hand. He said, "There may be a difference."

"Don't keep it from me."

"I think that Belloq's medallion had markings on one side only."

"Are you sure?"

"I'm reasonably sure."

"Now," Indy said, "all I need to know is what the markings mean."

"Then we should go to the house of Imam. We should go now."

Indy said nothing. Followed by Sallah, he left the courtyard and stepped out into the alley. He felt an urgency now. The Ark, yeah—but it was more than just the Ark now. It was for Marion. If her death was to make any sense, he had to get to the Well of the Souls before Belloq.

If death could ever make sense, he thought.

They climbed into Sallah's truck, and as they did, Indy noticed the monkey in the back. He stared at it. Wasn't it ever going to be possible to lose the thing? Pretty soon it would get around to learning human speech and calling him Dad. A echo in there caused him pain: Marion's little joke about the creature having his looks.

The monkey chattered and rubbed its forepaws.

After the truck had gone a little way, the motorcycle emerged from the darkness and followed.

The house of Imam was located on the outskirts of Cairo, built on a slight rise; it was an unusual construction, reminding Indy a little of an observatory. Indeed, as he and Sallah, followed by the monkey, walked toward the entranceway, he noticed an opening in the roof of the house from which there emerged a large telescope.

Sallah said, "Imam has many interests, Indiana. Priest. Scholar. Astronomer. If anyone can explain the markings, he can."

Ahead, the front door was opened. A young boy stood there, nodding his head as they entered.

"Good evening, Abu," Sallah said. "This is Indiana Jones." A brief, courteous introduction. "Indiana, this is Abu, Imam's apprentice."

Indy nodded, smiled, impatient to meet the scholar —who appeared at that moment at the end of the hallway. An old man in threadbare robes, his hands gnarled and covered with the brown spots of age; his eyes, though, were lit with curiosity and life. He bowed his head in a silent greeting. They followed him into his study, a large room strewn with manuscripts, pillows, maps, ancient documents. You could feel it here, Indy thought: a lifetime of dedication to the pursuit of knowledge. Every moment of every day a learning experience. Nothing wasted. Indy passed the medallion to Imam, who took it silently and carried it to a table at the back of the room where a small lamp was lit. He sat down, twisting the thing between his fingers, squinting at it. Indy and Sallah sat down on some cushions, the monkey between them. Sallah stroked the creature's neck.

Silence.

The old man took a sip of wine, then wrote something quickly on a small piece of paper. Indy twisted around, watching impatiently. It seemed Imam was examining the headpiece as if time were of no interest to him.

"Patience," Sallah said.

Hurry, Indy thought.

The man parked his motorcycle some way from the house. He slipped alongside the house to its rear, looking in windows until he found the kitchen. He pressed himself close to the wall, watching the boy, Abu, rinse some dates at the sink. He waited. Abu put the dates in a bowl, then placed the bowl on the table. Still the man didn't move, more shadow now than substance. The boy picked up a decanter of wine, several glasses, placed them on a tray, then left the kitchen. Only then did the man move out of the shadows. He took a bottle from his cloak, opened it, and, after looking around the kitchen, stealthily poured some liquid from the bottle over the bowl of dates. He paused for a second. He heard the sound of the boy returning, and quickly, as silently as he entered, he slipped away again.

Imam still hadn't spoken. Indy occasionally looked at Sallah, whose expression was that of a man accustomed to periods of enormous patience, periods of waiting. The door opened. Abu came in with a decanter of wine and glasses and set the tray down on the table. The wine was tempting, but Indy didn't move for it. He found the silence unsettling. The boy went out and when he next came back he was carrying food—plates of cheese, fruit, a bowl of dates. Sallah absently picked at a piece of cheese and chewed on it thoughtfully. The dates looked good, but Indy wasn't hungry. The monkey moved away, settling beneath the table. Silence still. Indy leaned forward and picked up one of the dates. He tilted his head back, tossed the date in the air and tried to catch it in his mouth as it fell—but it struck the edge of his chin and bounced away across the floor. Abu gave him a strange look—as if this Western custom were too insane to fathom—then picked up the date and dropped it in an ashtray.

Hell, Indy thought. My coordination must be shot.

"Look. Come over here and look," Imam suddenly said.

His strange hoarse voice broke the silence with the solemn authority of a prayer. It was the kind of voice to which one responded without thinking twice.

Over his shoulder, Indy and Sallah watched Imam point to the raised markings. "This is a warning . . . not to disturb the Ark of the Covenant."

"Just what I need," Indy said.

He bent forward, almost touching the frail shoulders of Imam.

"The other markings concern the height of the Staff of Ra to which this headpiece must be attached. Otherwise, the headpiece by itself is of no use." Indy noticed the old man's lips were faintly blackened, that he rubbed them time and again with his tongue.

"Then Belloq got the height of the Staff from his copy of the medallion," Indy said.

Sallah nodded.

"What do the markings say?" Indy asked.

"This was the old way. This means six kadam high."

"About seventy-two inches," Sallah said.

Indy heard the monkey moving around the food table, picking at assorted bits and pieces. He went over and picked up a date, grabbing it before the monkey reached it.

"I am not finished," Imam said. "On the other side of the headpiece there is more. I'll read it to you. 'And give back one kadam to honor the Hebrew God whose Ark this is.' "

Indy's hand stopped halfway to his mouth. "You're sure Belloq's medallion has markings on one side only?" he asked Sallah.

"Positive."

Indy started to laugh. "Then Belloq's staff is twelve inches too long! They're digging in the wrong spot!"

Sallah laughed too. The men hugged one another as Imam watched them, unsmiling.

The old man said, "I do not understand who Belloq is. I can only tell you that the warning about the Ark is a serious one. I can also tell you that it is written . . . those who would open the Ark and release its force will die if they look upon it. If they bring themselves face to face with it. I would heed these warnings, my friends."

It should have been a solemn moment, but Indy was suddenly too elated at the realization of the Frenchman's error to absorb the old man's words. A triumph! he thought. Wonderful. He wished he could see the look on Belloq's face when he couldn't find the Well of the Souls. He tossed a date in the air, opening his mouth.

This time, he thought.

But Sallah's hand picked the date out of the air before it could enter Indy's mouth.

"Hey!"

Sallah gestured toward the floor under the table.

The monkey lay there in a posture of death. It lay surrounded by date pits. Faintly one paw flickered, trembled, then the animal's eyes closed slowly. After that it didn't move again.

Indy turned his face toward Sallah.

The Egyptian shrugged and said, "Bad dates."

9: The Tanis Digs, Egypt

The desert morning was burning, the stretches of sand shimmering. A landscape, Indy thought, in which a man would have every right to claim he saw mirages. He stared at the sky as the truck rattled along the road. He was uncomfortable in the burnoose he'd borrowed from Sallah, and he wasn't entirely convinced that he could pass himself off as an Arab anyhow—but anything was worth a shot. He turned around from time to time to look at the other truck that followed. Sallah's friend Omar drove the second truck; in the back of it were six Arab diggers. There were another three in Sallah's truck. Let's hope, he thought, that they're as trustworthy as Sallah says.

"I am nervous," Sallah said. "I do not mind confessing it."

"Don't worry too much."

"You're taking a huge risk," Sallah said.

"That's the name of this game," Indy remarked. He looked up at the sky again. The early sunlight beat the sands with the force of a raging hammer.

Sallah sighed. "I hope we cut the staff to the correct size."

"We measured it pretty well," Indy said. He thought of the five-foot stick that lay right then in the back of the truck. It had taken them several hours last night to cut the thing, to whittle the end so that the headpiece would fit. A strange feeling, Indy thought, placing the medallion on the stick. He had felt a sharp affinity with the past then, imaging other hands placing the same medallion in exactly that way so long ago.

The two trucks came to a halt now. Indy got out and walked back to the truck driven by Omar; the Arab stepped down, raising his arm in greeting. And then he pointed to a spot in the distance, a place where the terrain was less flat, where sand dunes undulated.

"We will wait there," Omar said.

Indy rubbed his dry lips with the back of his hand.

"And good luck," the Arab said.

Omar got back into his truck and drove away, trailing a storm of dust and sand behind the vehicle. Indy watched it go. He went back to where Sallah was parked, climbed in; the truck moved slowly for a mile or so, then it stopped again. Sallah and Indy got out, crossed a strip of sand, then lay down and looked across a depression in the land beneath them.

The Tanis excavations.

It was elaborate, extensive; it was obvious, from the amount of equipment below, the numbers of workers, that the Führer wanted the Ark badly. There were trucks, bulldozers, tents. There were hundreds of Arab diggers and, it seemed, just as many German supervisors, incongruous in their uniforms somehow, as if they deliberately sought discomfort out here in the desert. The land had been dug, holes excavated, then abandoned, foundations and passageways unearthed and then deserted. And beyond the main digs was something that appeared to be a crude airstrip.

"I've never seen a dig this size," Indy said.

Sallah was pointing toward the center of the activity, indicating a large mound of sand, a hole at its core; a rope had been slung around it, suspended between posts.

"The Map Room," he said.

"What time does the sun hit it?"

"Just after eight."

"We don't have much time." He looked at the wristwatch he'd borrowed from Sallah. "Where are the Germans digging for the Well of the Souls?"

Sallah pointed again. Some way beyond the main activity, out in the dunes, were several trucks and a bulldozer. Indy watched for a while. Then he stood up. "You've got the rope?"

"Of course."

"Then let's go."

One of the Arab diggers took the wheel of the truck and drove it slowly toward the digs. Between the tents Indy and Sallah got out. They moved stealthily toward the Map Room, Indy carrying the five-foot staff and wondering how long he could contrive to be inconspicuous with so long a piece of wood in his hand. They passed several uniformed Germans, who hardly paid any attention to them: they were grouped together, smoking and talking in the morning sunlight. When they had gone a little further, Sallah indicated that they should stop: they had reached the Map Room. Indy looked around for a moment and then walked, as casually as he could, toward the edge of the hole—the ceiling of the ancient Map Room. He peered down inside, held his breath, and then looked at Sallah, who produced a length of rope from under his robes and tied one end of it around an oil drum located nearby. Indy lowered the staff inside the hole, smiled at Sallah and took one end of the rope. Sallah watched grimly, face covered in perspiration. Indy began to lower himself inside the Map Room.

The Map Room at Tanis, he thought. At some other time he might have been awed by the mere thought of actually being in this place; at some other time he might have paused to look around, might have wanted to linger—but not now. He reached the floor and tugged on the rope, which was immediately pulled up. Damned hard, he thought, not to get excited by this place—an elaborate frescoed room lit by the sunlight streaming in from overhead. He moved across the floor to where the miniature model of the city of Tanis was laid out: a remarkable map cut out of stone, immaculate in detail, so well constructed you could almost imagine miniature people existing in those buildings or walking those streets. He couldn't help but be astonished by the craftsmanship of the map, the patience that must have gone into the construction.

Alongside the map was a line created by embedded mosaic tiles. There were evenly spaced slots in this line, each accompanied by a symbol for a time of the year. The slots had been made to accommodate the base of the staff. He took the headpiece from his robes, reached for the staff and looked at the reflected sunlight that had already begun to move slowly across the miniature city at his feet.

It was seven-fifty. He didn't have much time.

Sallah had gathered the rope, bunched it in his hands and begun to move back toward the oil drum. He barely heard the jeep that came up alongside him, and the loud voice of the German startled him.

"Hey! You!"

Sallah tried to smile dumbly.

The German said, "You, right. What are you doing there?"

"Nothing, nothing." He inclined his head in a gesture of innocence.

"Bring that rope over here," the German said. "This damn jeep is stuck."

Sallah hesitated, then he untied the rope and carried it toward the jeep. Already another vehicle, a truck, had appeared; it stopped some feet in front of the jeep.

"Tie the rope from the jeep to the truck," the German said.

Sallah, sweating, did so. The rope, he thought: the precious rope is being tugged away. He listened to the engines of the two vehicles, watching the wheels squirm in the sand. The rope was pulled taut. What was he going to do to get Indy out of the Map Room without a rope?

He followed the jeep a little way across the sand, failing to notice he was standing beside a kettle of hot food cooking over an open flame. There were several German soldiers seated around a table and one of them was calling to him to bring some food. Helplessly, he watched the German.

"Are you deaf?"

He bowed subserviently and lifted the heavy kettle, carrying it toward the table. What he was thinking about was Indy trapped in the Map Room; what he was wondering about was how, without a rope, he could get the American out.

He began to serve, trying to ignore the insults of the soldiers. He served hurriedly. He spilled food across the table and was cuffed around the side of the head for his efforts.

"Clumsy! Look at my shirt. Look what you've spilled on my shirt."

Sallah lowered his face. Mock shame.

"Get some water. Hurry."

He rushed away to find water.

Indy took the headpiece and fitted it carefully to the top of the staff. He placed the base of the staff in one of the mosaic slots and listened to the sound of the wood clicking against the ancient tile. The sunlight caught the top of the headpiece, the yellow beam moving within a fraction of the tiny hole in the crystal. He waited. From overhead he could hear the sounds of voices shouting. He blocked them out. Later, if he had to, he'd worry about the Germans. But not now.

The sunlight pierced the crystal, throwing a bright line across the miniature city. The line of light was altered and broken by the prism of the crystal—and there, in those miniature buildings and streets, it fell across one spot in particular. Red light, glowing against a small building, which, as if by some ancient chemistry, some old artistry, began to glow. In amazement he watched this effect, noticing now some markings of red paint among the other buildings, markings that were fresh and clean. *Belloq's calculations.*

Or *mis*calculations: the building illuminated by the headpiece was eighteen inches closer than the last red mark left by the Frenchman.

Terrific. Perfect. He couldn't have hoped for anything better. Indy went down on his knees beside the miniature city and took a tape measure from his robes. He strung the tape between Belloq's last mark and the building glowing in sunlight. He made his calculations quickly, scribbling on a small notepad. Sweat burned on his face, dripped across the backs of his hands.

Sallah didn't go for water. He scampered between tents, hoping none of the Germans would stop him again. Panicked, he began to look for a rope. He didn't find one. No rope, nothing in sight. He scurried here and there, slipping and sliding in the sand, praying that none of the Germans would notice his peculiar behavior or call on him to perform some menial task. He had to do something fast to get Indy out. But what?

He paused. Between a couple of tents lay several hampers, their lids open.

No rope, he thought; so in such circumstances you improvise.

When he'd made sure he wasn't being watched, he moved toward the hampers.

Indy snapped the wooden staff in two and stuck the headpiece back into his robes. He placed the pieces of wood in a far corner of the Map Room, then he went to a spot directly under the hole and stared upward at the bright sky. The brilliant blue blinded him momentarily.

"Sallah," he called out, caught between a shout and a whisper.

Nothing.

"Sallah."

Nothing.

He glanced around the room for an alternative way

out, but there wasn't one as far as he could see. Where was Sallah?

"Sallah!"

Silence.

He watched the opening; he blinked against the harsh light, waited.

There was a sudden movement above. Then something began to fall from the hole and for a second he thought it was the rope, but it wasn't: instead, what he saw descending was a bunch of clothing tied together, clumsily knotted to create a makeshift rope—shirts, tunics, pants, robes and—of all things—a swastika flag.

He caught hold of the line, tugged on it, and then began to climb. He surfaced, dropping flat on his stomach as Sallah started to haul the line of clothing out. Indy smiled and the Egyptian stuffed the makeshift rope inside the oil drum. Then Indy rose and followed Sallah quickly between some tents.

They didn't see the German who was walking up and down with an expression of dark impatience on his face.

"You! I'm still waiting for that water!"

Sallah spread his hands apologetically.

The German turned to Indy. "You're another lazy bastard. Why aren't you digging?"

Sallah moved toward the German while Indy, bowing in wonderful subservience, hurried off in the other direction.

He moved quickly now, his robes flapping as he rushed between tents. And from behind, as if some suspicion had just been aroused, some crime suspected, he could hear the German calling after him. *Wait. Come back here.* Indy thought; The last thing I intend to do is come back, dummkopf. He hurried along the tents, caught between his unwillingness to look suspicious and his urge to start digging for the Well of the Souls, when two German officers appeared ahead of him. Damn, he thought, pausing, watching them stop to talk, light cigarettes. His way was blocked.

He slipped along the sides of the tents, hugging such shadow as he could find, and then he moved through an opening, a doorway, and stepped inside one of the tents. He could wait here at least for a few minutes until the way was clear. Those two Krauts could hardly stand out there smoking and talking all day.

He wiped sweat from his forehead, rubbed the damp palms of his hands against his robes. For the first time since he'd entered the place, he considered the Map Room: he thought of that weird sense of timelessness he'd felt, an experience of being somehow suspended, afloat—as if he himself had become a trapped object in the jar of history, preserved, perfect, intact. The Map Room at Tanis. In a way it was like discovering that a fairy tale had some basis in reality—the legend at the heart of which there is truth. The thought touched him in a fashion he found a little humbling: you live in the year 1936, with its airplanes and its radios and its great machines of war—and then you stumble across something so simply intricate, so primitively elaborate, as a miniature map with one specific building designed to glow when struck by light in a certain way. Call it alchemy, artistry or even magic—however you cut it, the passage of centuries hadn't improved anything very much. The movement of time had merely slashed at the roots of some profound sense of the cosmic, the magical.

And now he was within reach of the Well of the Souls.

The Ark.

He wiped his forehead again with the edge of his robes. He peered through the slit in the tent. They were still there, smoking, talking. When the hell would they find a reason to move on?

He was pondering a way out, trying to think up a means of making an exit, when he heard a noise from the other corner of the tent. A strange grunting, a stifled noise. He turned around and peered across the tent, which he had convinced himself was empty.

For a moment, a moment of disbelief, wild incredulity, he felt all his pulses stammer and stop.

She was sitting in a chair, tied to it by crisscrossing ropes, a handkerchief bound tightly around her mouth. She was sitting there, her eyes imploring him, flashing messages at him, and she was trying to speak to him through the folds of the handkerchief pressed against her lips. He crossed the floor quickly, untied the gag and let it fall from her mouth. He kissed her and the kiss was anxious, long, deep. When he pulled his face away, he laid the palm of his hand flat against her cheek.

When she spoke her voice faltered. "They had two baskets . . . two baskets to confuse you. When you thought I was in the truck I was in a car . . ."

"I thought you were dead," he said. What was that sensation he felt now—unfathomable relief? the lifting of guilt? Or was it pure pleasure, gratitude, that she was still alive?

"I'm still kicking," she said.

"Have they hurt you?"

She seemed to struggle with some inner anxiety. "No—they haven't hurt me. They just asked about you, they wanted to find out what you knew."

Indy rubbed his jaw and wondered why he detected an odd hesitation in Marion. But he was still too excited to pause and consider it.

"Indy, please get me away from here. He's evil—"

"Who?"

"The Frenchman."

He was about to untie the rope when he stopped.

"What's wrong?" she asked.

"Look, you'll never understand how I feel right now. I'll never be able to find words for that. But I want you to trust me. I'm going to do something I don't like doing."

"Untie me, Indy. Please untie me."

"That's the point. If I let you loose, then they're going to turn over every particle of sand around here to find you and I can't afford that right now. And since I know where the Ark is, it's important I get to it before they do, then I can come back for you—"

"Indy, no!"

"You only need to sit tight for a little longer—"

"You bastard. Turn me loose!"

He slipped the gag back over her mouth and tightened it. Then, kissing her once more on the forehead, ignoring her protests, her grunts, he stood upright. "Sit tight," he said. "I'll be back."

I'll be back, he thought. There was a very old echo there, an echo that went back ten years. And he could see doubt in her eyes. He kissed her again, then moved toward the opening in the tent.

She thumped her chair on the floor.

He went outside; the German officers had gone.

Overhead, the sun was stronger now. It beat down insanely.

Alive, he thought: she's alive. And the thought was something that soared inside his head. He began to rush, moving away from the tents, from the excavations, out into the burning dunes, out into that place where he had a rendezvous with Omar and his diggers.

He took the surveyor's instrument from the back of Omar's truck and erected it on the dunes. He aligned it with the Map Room in the distance, and consulting the calculations he had made, he got a fix on a position some miles out in the desert, out in untouched sand considerably closer than the spot where Belloq was mistakenly digging for the Well of the Souls. *There,* he thought. The exact place!

"Got it!" he said, and he folded the instrument and stuck it back in the truck. The place was well hidden from Belloq's dig, concealed by the rise of the dunes. They could dig unobserved.

As he was climbing into the truck, Indy noticed a figure appear over the dunes. It was Sallah, robes flapping, hurrying toward the truck.

"I thought you were never coming," Indy said.

"I almost didn't," Sallah said, climbing in back.

"Let's go," Indy told the driver.

When they had gone out into the dunes they parked the truck. It was a barren spot in which to be looking for something so exciting as the Ark. Overhead the sun was incandescent, the color of an exploding yellow rose; and that was what it suggested in its intensity, a thing about to burst loose from the sky.

They went to the spot which Indy had calculated. For a short time he stood and stared at it—dry sand. You could never dream of anything growing here. You could never imagine this ground yielding up anything. Certainly not the Ark.

Indy went to the truck and took out a shovel. The diggers were already moving toward the spot. They had leathery faces, burned faces. Indy wondered if they managed to live beyond forty in a place like this.

Sallah, carrying a spade, walked alongside him. "I believe they might come here only if Belloq realizes he's working in the wrong place. Otherwise, there would be no good reason."

"Who ever heard of a Nazi needing a good reason?"

Sallah smiled. He turned and gazed across the dunes; miles of nothing stretched away. He was silent for a moment. Then he said, "Even a Nazi would need a good reason to wander in this place."

Indy struck the ground with the point of his spade. "He'd still need a requisition and have it signed in triplicate in Berlin." He looked at the diggers. "Let's go," he said. "Let's get on with this."

They began their dig, heaping sand, laboring hard, furiously, pausing only to drink water that had already turned warm in the camel-skin bags. They dug until the light had gone from the sky; but the same heat remained, tethered to the sand.

Belloq sat in his tent, drumming his fingertips on the table that held maps, drawings of the Ark, sheets of paper covered with the hieroglyphics of his calculations. There was a dark mood of frustration inside him; he was edgy, nervous—and the presence of Dietrich, as well as Dietrich's lackey Gobler, didn't help his frame of mind much. Belloq rose, went to a washbasin, splashed water across his face.

"A wasted day," Dietrich said. "A wasted day . . ."

Belloq toweled his face, then poured himself a small shot of cognac. He stared at the German, then at the underling Gobler, who seemed to exist only as a shadow of Dietrich.

Dietrich, undeterred, went on: "My men have been digging all day—and for what? Tell me, for what?"

Belloq sipped his drink, then said, "Based on the information in my possession, my calculations were correct. But archaeology is not the most exact of sciences, Dietrich. I don't think you entirely understand this fact. Perhaps the Ark will be found in an adjoining chamber. Perhaps some vital piece of evidence still eludes us." He shrugged and finished his drink. Usually he loathed the way the Germans nit-picked, the way they always seemed to hover around him as if they expected him to be a seer, a prophet. Now, however, he understood their change in mood.

"The Führer demands constant reports of progress," Dietrich said. "He is not a patient man."

"You may cast your mind back to my conversation with your Führer, Dietrich. You may well recall I made no promises. I simply said that things looked favorable, nothing more."

There was a silence. Gobler moved in front of the kerosene lamp, throwing a huge shadow that Belloq found curiously menacing. Gobler said, "The girl could help us. After all, she was in possession of the original piece for years."

"Indeed," Dietrich said.

"I doubt if she knows anything," Belloq said.

"It is worth a try," Gobler said.

He wondered why he found their treatment of the girl so unsettling to him. They had used her barbarically—they had threatened her with a variety of tortures, but it seemed apparent to him that she had nothing to tell. Was this some soft spot, some awful weakness, he had toward her? The thought appalled him. He stared at Dietrich for a moment. How very badly they live in fear of their sorry little Führer, he thought. He must strut through their dreams at night —if they dreamed at all, a prospect he couldn't quite believe. They were men stripped of imagination.

"If you don't want to be concerned with the girl, Belloq, I have someone who can undertake the task of discovering what she knows."

It was no time to parade a weakness, a concern for the woman. Dietrich went to the opening of the tent and called out. After a moment the man named Arnold Toht appeared, extending his arm in a Nazi salute. In the center of his palm was the scar, burned-out tissue, in the perfect shape of the headpiece.

"The woman," Dietrich said. "I believe you know her, Toht."

Toht said, "There are old scores to settle."

"And old scars," Belloq said.

Toht self-consciously lowered his hand.

When it was dark and a pale desert moon had come up over the horizon, a moon of muted blue, Indy and his Arabs stopped digging. They had lit torches, watching the moon begin slowly to darken as clouds passed in front of it; after that there was lightning in the sky, strange lightning that came in brief forks and flashes, an electric storm summoned, it seemed, out of nowhere.

The men had dug a hole that revealed a heavy stone door flush with the bottom of the pit. For a long time nobody said anything. Tools were produced from the truck and the diggers forced the stone door open, grunting as they labored with the weight of the thing.

The stone door was pulled back. Beneath the door was an underground chamber. *The Well of the Souls.* It was about thirty feet deep, a large chamber whose walls were covered with hieroglyphics and carvings. The roof of the place was supported by huge statues, guardians of the vault. It was an awesome construction, and it created, in the light of the torches, a sense of bottomlessness, an abyss in which history itself was trapped. The men moved their torches as they peered down.

The far end of the chamber came into view, barely lit. There was a stone altar that held a stone chest; a floor covered with some form of strange dark carpeting.

"The chest must contain the Ark," Indy said. "I don't understand what that gray stuff is all over the floor."

But then, in another flash of lightning, he saw; he shook, dropping his torch down into the Well, hearing the hiss of hundreds of snakes.

As the torch burned, the snakes moved away from the heart of the flame. More than hundreds, thousands of snakes, Egyptian asps, shivering and undulating and coiling across the floor as they answered the flame with their savage hissing. The floor seemed to move in the flicker of the torch—but it wasn't the floor, it was the snakes, striking backward from the flame. Only the altar was untouched by snakes. Only the stone altar seemed immune to the asps.

"Why did it have to be snakes?" Indy asked. "Anything but snakes, anything else. I could have taken almost anything else."

"Asps," Sallah said. "Very poisonous."

"Thanks for that piece of news, Sallah."

"They stay clear of the flame, you notice."

Pull yourself together, Indy thought. You're so close to the Ark you can *feel* it, so you face your phobia head on and do something about it. A thousand snakes—so what? So what? The living floor was the embodiment of an old nightmare. Snakes pursued him in the darkest of his dreams, rooting around his innermost fears. He turned to the diggers and said, "Okay. Okay. A few snakes. Big deal. I want lots of torches. And oil. I want a landing strip down there."

After a time, lit torches were dropped into the Well.

Several canisters of oil were dropped into the spaces where the snakes had slithered away from the flames. The diggers then began to lower a large wooden crate, rope handles attached to each corner, into the hole. Indy watched, wondering if a phobia were something you could swallow, digest, something you could ignore as though it were the intense pain of a passing indigestion. Despite his resolve to go down there, he shuddered—and the asps, coiling and uncoiling, filled the darkness with their sibilant sound, a sound more menacing than any he'd ever heard. A rope was lowered now: he stood upright, swallowed hard, then swung out on the rope and down into the Well. A moment later Sallah followed him. Beyond the edges of the flames the snakes wriggled, slid, snakes piled on snakes, mountains of the reptiles, snake eggs hatching, shells breaking to reveal tiny asps, snakes devouring other snakes.

For a time he hung suspended, the rope swaying back and forth, Sallah hanging just above him.

"I guess this is it," he said.

Marion watched as Belloq entered the tent. He came across the floor slowly and studied her for a while, but he made no move to untie her gag. What was it about this man? What was it that caused a sensation, something almost like panic, inside her? She could hear the sound of her heart beat. She stared at him, wishing she could just close her eyes and turn her face away. When she had first met him after being captured, he had said very little to her—he had simply scrutinized her in the way he was doing now. The eyes were cold and yet they seemed capable, although she wasn't sure how she knew this, of yielding to occasional warmth. They were also knowing, as if he had gone far into some profound secret, as if he had tested reality and found it lacking. The face was handsome in the way she might have associated with pictures in romantic magazines of Europeans wearing white suits and sipping exotic drinks on the terraces of villas. But these weren't the qualities that touched her.

Something else.

Something she didn't want to think about.

Now she closed her eyes. Marion couldn't bear to be so closely stared at, she couldn't bear to think of herself as an object of scrutiny—perhaps like some archaeological fragment, a sliver of clay broken loose from the jigsaw of an ancient piece of pottery. Inanimate, a thing to be classified.

When she heard him move she opened her eyes.

He still didn't speak. And her uneasiness grew. He moved across the floor until he was standing directly over her, then he put his hand forward very slowly and slipped the gag from her lips, sliding it softly and teasingly from her mouth. She had a sudden picture, one she didn't want to entertain, of his hand caressing the fold of her hip. No, she thought. It isn't like that at all. But the image remained in her head. And Belloq's hand, with the certainty of the successful lover, gently drew the gag from her mouth to her chin and then he was untying the knot—everything performed slowly, with the kind of casual elegance of a seducer who senses, in some predatory way, the yielding of his prey.

She twisted her head to the side. She wanted to cut these thoughts off, but she seemed incapable of doing it. I don't want to be attracted to this man, she thought. I don't want him to touch me. But then, as he moved his fingers beneath her chin and began to stroke her throat, she realized she was incapable of fighting. I won't let him see it in my eyes, she told herself. I won't let him see this in my face. Despite herself, she began to imagine his hands drifting across the surface of her body, hands that were strangely gentle, considerate in their touches, intimate and exciting in their promises. And suddenly she knew that this man would make a lover of extraordinary unselfishness, that he would bring out of her the kind of pleasures she hadn't ever experienced before.

He knows it, she thought. He knows it, too.

He brought his face close. She could smell the sweetness of his breath. No no no, she thought. But she didn't speak. She knew she was leaning forward slightly, anticipating the kiss, her mind dancing, her desire intense. It didn't come. There wasn't a kiss. He had bent down and was beginning to untie her ropes, moving in the same way as before, letting the ropes fall to the ground as if they were the most erotic of garments.

Still he hadn't spoken.

He was looking at her. There was a light in his eye, the faint touch of warmth she'd imagined before —but she couldn't tell if it was real or if it was something he used, a prop in his repertoire of behavior.

Then he said, "You're very beautiful."

She shook her head. "Please . . ." But she didn't know if she was begging to be left alone or if she was asking him to kiss her, and she realized she'd never experienced such a confusion of emotion in her entire life. Indy; why the hell hadn't he rescued her? Why had he left her like this?

Repelled, attracted—why wasn't there some hard and fast borderline between the two? Signposts she could read? It didn't matter: there was a melting of distinctions in her thoughts. She saw the contradiction and she understood, with a sense of horror, that she wanted this man to make love to her, to teach her what she felt was his deep understanding of physical love; and beyond this, there was the feeling that he could be cruel, an insight that suddenly didn't matter to her either.

He brought his face closer again. She looked at his lips. The eyes were filled with understanding, a comprehension she hadn't seen in a man's face before. Already, even before he kissed her, he knew her, he could look into her. She felt more naked than she'd ever felt. Even this vulnerability excited her now. He came nearer. He kissed her.

She wanted to draw away again.

The kiss—she closed her eyes and gave herself to

the kiss—and it wasn't like any other kiss in her life. It moved into a place beyond the narrow limits of lips and tongues. It created spaces of bright light in her head, colors, webs of gold and silver and yellow and blue, as if she were watching some impossible sunset. Slow, patient, unselfish. Nobody had ever touched her before. Not like that. Not even Indy.

When he drew his face away, she realized she was holding him tightly. She was digging her nails into his body. And the realization came as a shock to her, a shock that brought a sudden sense of shame. What was she doing? What had possessed her?

She stepped back from him.

"Please," she said. "No more."

He smiled and spoke for the first time: "They intend to harm you."

It was as if the kiss had never existed. It was as if she had been manipulated. The abrupt letdown she experienced was the wild drop in a roller-coaster ride.

"I managed to persuade them to give me some time alone with you, my dear. You're a very attractive woman, after all. And I don't want to see them hurt you. They're barbarians."

He came closer to her again. No, she thought. Not again.

"You must tell me something to placate them. Some information."

"I don't know anything . . . how many times do I have to tell them?" She was dizzy now, she needed to sit down. Why didn't he kiss her again?

"What about Jones?"

"I don't know anything."

"Your loyalty is admirable. But you must tell me what Jones knows."

Indy came swimming back into her vision.

"He's brought me nothing but trouble . . . "

"I agree," Belloq said. He reached for her, held her face between his hands, studied her eyes. "I think I want to believe you know nothing. But I cannot control the Germans. I cannot hold them back."

"Don't let them hurt me."

Belloq shrugged. "Then tell me *anything*!"

The tent door flapped open. Marion looked at the figure of Arnold Toht standing there. Behind him were the Germans she had come to know as Dietrich and Gobler. The fear she felt was like some sun burning in her head.

Belloq said, "I'm sorry."

She didn't move. She simply stared at Toht, remembering how badly he'd wanted to hurt her with the poker.

"Fräulein," Toht said. "We have come a long way from Nepal, no?"

Stepping backward, she shook her head in fear.

Toht advanced toward her. She glanced at Belloq, as if to make some last appeal to him, but he was going from the tent now, stepping out into the night.

Outside, Belloq paused. It was odd to be attracted by the woman, strange to want to make love to her even if the act had begun out of the desire to extract information from her. But after that, after the first kiss . . . He stuck his hands in his pockets and hesitated outside the tent. He wanted to go back inside and make those worms stop what they were about to do, but his attention was suddenly drawn to the horizon.

Lightning—lightning concentrated strangely in one place, as if it had gathered there deliberately, directed by some meteorological consciousness. A congregation of lightning, spikes and forks and flashes spitting in one spot. He bit on his lower lip, deep in thought, and then he went back inside the tent.

Indy moved toward the altar. He tried to ignore the sound of the snakes, a mad noise—made more insane by the eerie shadows thrown by the torches. He had splashed oil from the canisters across the floor and lit it, creating a path among the snakes; and now these flames, thrusting upward, eclipsed the lightning from overhead. Sallah was behind him. Together they struggled with the stone cover of the chest until it was loose; inside, more beautiful than he'd ever imagined it to be, was the Ark.

For a time he couldn't move. He stared at the untarnished gold angels that faced one another over the lid, the gold that coated the acacia wood. The gold carrying-rings affixed to the four corners shone brilliantly in the light of his torch. He looked at Sallah, who was watching the Ark in reverential silence. More than anything else now Indy had the urge to reach out and touch the Ark—but even as he thought it, Sallah put his hand forward.

"Don't touch it," Indy exclaimed. "Never touch it."

Sallah drew his hand away. They turned toward the wooden crate and removed the four poles that were attached to the corners. They inserted the poles into the rings of the Ark and raised it, grunting at the weight of the thing, then levering it from the stone chest into the crate. The fires were beginning to die now and the snakes, their hissing beginning to sound more and more like a solitary upraised voice, were slipping toward the altar.

"Hurry," Indy said. "Hurry."

They attached the ropes to the crate. Indy tugged on one of the ropes, and the crate was pulled up out of the chamber. Sallah took the next rope and quickly made his ascent. Indy reached for his exit rope, pulling on it to be certain of its support—and it *fell,* itself snakelike, from the opening at the top into the chamber.

"What the hell—"

From above, the Frenchman's voice was unmistakable: "Why, Dr. Jones, whatever are you doing in such a nasty place?"

There was laughter.

'You're making a habit of this, Belloq," Indy said.

The snakes hissed closer. He could hear their bodies slide across the floor.

"A bad habit, I agree," Belloq said, peering down. "Unhappily, I have no further use for you, my old friend. And I find it suitably ironic that you're about to become a permanent addition to this archaeological find."

"I'm dying of laughter," Indy shouted up.

He continued to squint upward, wondering if there were any exit from this . . . and he was still wondering when he saw Marion being pushed from the edge of the hole, falling, dropping. He moved quickly and broke her fall with his body, sliding to the ground as she struck him. The snakes edged closer. She clung frantically to Indy, who could hear Belloq arguing from above.

"She was mine!"

"She is of no use to us now, Belloq. Only the mission for the Führer matters."

"I had plans for her!"

"The only plans are those that concern Berlin," Dietrich said back to Belloq.

There was a silence from above. And then Belloq was looking down into the chamber at Marion.

His voice was low. "It was not to be," he said to her. Then he nodded at Indy. "Indiana Jones, *adieu!*"

Suddenly the stone door to the chamber was slammed shut by a group of German soldiers. Air was sucked out of the Well, torches went out, and the snakes were moving into the areas of darkness.

Marion clutched Indy tightly. He disentangled himself, picking up two torches that were still lit, passing one to her.

"Just wave the torch at anything that moves," he said.

"*Everything* is moving," she said. "The whole place is slithering."

"Don't remind me."

He began to fumble around in the dark, found one of the oil canisters, splashed the oil toward the wall and lit it. He stared at one of the statues above, feeling the snakes encroach ever closer to him.

"What are you doing?" Marion asked.

He poured what remained of the oil in a circle around them and set it ablaze.

"Stay here."

"Why? Where are you going?"

"I'll be back. Keep your eyes open and get ready to run."

"Run where?"

He didn't answer. He moved backward through the flames to the center of the room. Snakes flicked around his heels, and he swung his torch desperately to keep them away. He stared up at the statue, which reached close to the ceiling. From under his robes he took his bullwhip and lashed it through the half-light, watching it curl around the base of the statue. He tugged on it to test its strength, then he began to climb one-handed, the torch in his other hand.

He hauled himself up and twisted once to look down at Marion, who stood behind the dwindling wall of flame. She looked lost and forlorn and helpless. He made it to the top of the statue when a snake appeared around the face of the statue—hissing directly into Indy's eyes. Indy shoved his torch into its head, smelled the burning of reptile flesh, watched the snake slip from the smooth stone and fall away.

He jammed himself in place, his feet stuck between wall and statue. *Let it work,* he thought. Snakes were climbing up around the statue, and his torch—failing badly—wouldn't keep them away forever. He flailed with it, striking this way and that, hearing snakes drop and fall into the chamber. Then the torch slipped from his grasp and flickered out as it dropped. Just when you need a light, you don't have one, he thought.

And something crawled over his hand.

He yelled in surprise.

As he did so, the statue gave way, came loose from its foundation and swayed, shivered, tilting at a terrifying angle to the roof of the chamber. Here we go, Indy thought, holding onto this statue as if it were a wild mule. But it was more like a log being clutched in a stormy sea—and it fell, it fell while he struggled to hold on, gathering speed, toppling past the startled Marion, who stood in the dying fires, whizzing past her in the manner of a tree felled by a lumberjack, breaking through the floor of the Well and crashing into darkness beyond. Then the voyage astride the statue stopped abruptly when the broken figure hit bottom, and he slid off, stunned, rubbing the side of his head. He fumbled around in the dark for a moment, aware of faint light filtering through the ragged hole from the Well. Marion was calling to him.

"Indy! Where are you?"

He reached through the hole as she peered into it.

"Never ride by statue," he said. "Take my advice."

"I'll make a point of it."

He caught her hand and helped her in. She held the torch over her head. It was a poor light now—but enough for them to see they were inside a maze of interconnected chambers running at angles beneath the Well, catacombs that tunneled the earth.

"So where are we now?"

"Your guess would be as good as mine. Maybe they built the Well above these catacombs for some reason. I don't know. It's hard to say. But it's better than snakes."

A swarm of distressed bats flew out of the dark, winging around them, beating the air like lunatics. They ducked and passed into another chamber. Marion flapped her hands over her head and screamed.

"Don't do that," he said. "It scares me."

"How do you think it makes *me* feel?"

They went from chamber to chamber.

"There has to be some way out," he said. "The bats are a good sign. They have to find the sky outside for feeding purposes."

Another chamber, and here the stench was sickening. Marion raised her torch.

There were moldering mummies in their half-wrapped bandages, rotting flesh hanging from yellowed bindings, mounds of skulls, bones, some of them with half-preserved flesh clinging to their surfaces. A wall in front of them was covered with glistening beetles.

"I can't believe this smell," Marion said.

"You're complaining?"

"I think I'm going to be sick."

"Great," Indy told her. "That'd cap this experience nicely."

Marion sighed. "This is the worst place I've ever been."

"No, *back there* was the worst place you've ever been."

"But you know what, Indy?" she said. "If I had to be here with anybody . . ."

"Got you," he cut her off. "Got you."

"That's right. You do."

Marion kissed him gently on the lips. The softness of her touch surprised him. He drew his face back, wanted to kiss her again—but she was pointing excitedly at something, and when he turned his face he saw, some distance away, the merciful sight of the desert sun, a dawn sun, white and wonderful and promising.

"Thank God," she said.

"Thank who you like. But we've still got work to do."

10: The Tanis Digs, Egypt

They moved among the abandoned excavations, closer to the airstrip that had been hacked out of the desert by the Germans. There were two fuel trucks on the strip, a tent supply depot, and someone—clearly a mechanic to judge from his coveralls—standing at the edge of the runway with his hands on his hips, his face turned toward the sky. And then someone else was moving across the strip toward the mechanic, a figure Marion recognized as Dietrich's aide, Gobler.

Abruptly, there was a roaring noise in the sky, and from their position behind the abandoned dig, Marion and Indy saw a Flying Wing make an approach to land.

Gobler was shouting at the mechanic: "Get it gassed up at once! It has to be ready to fly out immediately with an important cargo!"

The Flying Wing came down, bouncing along the strip.

"They're going to put the Ark on that plane," Indy said.

"So what do we do then? Wave good-bye?"

"No. When the Ark gets loaded, we'll already be on the plane."

She looked at him quizzically. "Another of your schemes?"

"We've come this far—let's keep going." They moved, scurrying to a place just behind the supply tent. The mechanic was already putting blocks in front of the tires of the Flying Wing. The German attached the fuel hose to the plane. The propellers were spinning, the engine still roaring in a deafening way.

They moved even closer to the strip now, neither of them seeing another German mechanic, a fair-haired young man with tattooed arms, come up behind them. He crept toward them with the wrench upraised, his target the base of Indy's skull. It was Marion who saw his shadow first, saw it fall in a blur in front of her; she shouted. Indy turned as the wrench started to drop. He sprang to his feet, grabbed the swinging arm and wrestled the man to the ground while Marion skipped away behind some crates, watching, wondering what she could do to help.

Indy and the man rolled out across the strip. The first mechanic moved away from the plane, stood over the two wrestling figures and waited for the chance to launch a kick at Indy—but then Indy was up, agile, turning on the first man and knocking him down with a two-fisted shot. But the man with the tattooed arms was still eager to fight, and they struggled together again, rolling toward the rear of the plane, where the reverse propellers were spinning in a crazy way.

You could be mincemeat any second now, Indy thought.

He could feel the vicious blades carve the air around him as daggers through butter.

He tried to push the young guy back from the props, but the kid was strong. Grunting, Indy caught the kid by the throat and pressed hard, but the German swung away and came back again with a renewed vitality. Marion, watching from the crates, saw the pilot climb out of his cockpit and take a Luger from his tunic, leveling it, looking for a clear shot at Indy. She rushed across the strip, heaved one of the tire blocks from under the wheels and struck the pilot on the side of the skull with it, and he went down, dropping back into the cockpit, settling on the throttle so that the engine revved even harder.

The plane began to roll, rotating as if frustrated around its only set of tires that were still blocked. Marion reached for the edge of the cockpit to keep from slipping into the props, then she bent inside and tried to push the unconscious pilot away from the throttle.

Nothing. He was too heavy. The plane was threatening to go out of control and tilt, probably squashing Indy, or cutting him to thin ribbons into the bargain. The things I do for you, Indy, she thought. And she stepped into the cockpit, striking the plexiglass shield, causing it to slide shut above her. Still the plane was swinging, the wing moving dangerously over the place where Indy was fighting with the German. Panicked, she saw him knock the man down, and then he was up once more only for Indy to punch him backward . . .

Into the propeller.

Marion shut her eyes. But not before she saw the blades carve through the young German, sending up a spray of blood. And still the plane was rolling. She opened her eyes, tried to get out of the cockpit, realized she was stuck. She hammered on the lid, but nothing happened. *First a basket, now a cockpit,* she thought. *Where does it end?*

Indy raced toward the plane, watching it tilt, shocked to see Marion hammering against the inside of the cockpit. Now the wing, breaking, tilting, sliced into the fuel truck, breaking it open with the final authority of a surgeon's knife, spilling fuel across the strip like blood from an anesthetized patient. Indy began to run, skidding over the gasoline. He struggled for balance, slipped, got up and began to run again. He leaped up onto the wing and clambered toward the cockpit.

"Get out! This whole thing's going to blow!" he shouted at her.

He reached for the clasp that would open the cockpit from the outside.

He forced it, struggled with it, assailed by the strong smell of fuel flowing from the truck.

Trapped, Marion watched him imploringly.

The wooden crate, surrounded by three armed German soldiers, stood outside the entrance to Dietrich's tent. Inside, in a flurry of activity, papers were being packed, maps folded, radio sets dismantled. Belloq, standing inside the tent, watched the preparation for departure in an absent-minded fashion. His mind was concerned entirely with what lay inside the crate, the very thing he could hardly wait to examine. It was hard to restrain his impatience, to keep himself in check. He was remembering now the ritual preparations that had to be observed when opening the Ark. It was strange how, through the years, he had been making himself ready for this time—and strange, too, to realize how familiar he had become with the incantations. The Nazis wouldn't like it, of course—but they could do what they wanted with the Ark after he'd finished with it. They could pack it off and store it in some godawful museum for all he cared.

Hebraic incantations: they wouldn't like that at all. And the thought caused him some amusement. But the amusement didn't last long because the contents of the crate once more drew his attention. If everything he had ever learned about the Ark was true, if all the old stories concerning its power were correct, he would be the first man to make direct communication with that which had its source in a place—an infinite place—beyond human understanding.

He stepped out of the tent.

In the distance, flaring like a column of fire that might have been directed from heaven, there was a vast explosion.

He realized it was coming from the airstrip.

He began to run, driven with anxiety, toward the strip.

Dietrich came up behind him, followed by Gobler, who'd been at the strip only several minutes ago.

The fuel trucks had exploded and the airplane was a fiery wreck.

"Sabotage," Dietrich said. "But who?"

"Jones," Belloq said.

"Jones?" Dietrich looked bewildered.

"The man has more lives than the proverbial cat," Belloq said. "But a time must come when he has used them all up, no?"

They watched the flames in silence.

"We must get the Ark away from here at once," Belloq said. "We must put it on a truck and go to Cairo. We can fly from there."

Belloq stared a moment longer at the carnage, wondering at Indiana Jones's sense of purpose, his lavish gift of survival. One had to admire the man's tenacious hold on life. And one had to beware of the cunning, the fortitude, that lay behind it. It was always possible, Belloq thought, to underestimate the opposition. And perhaps all along he had underestimated Indiana Jones.

"We must have plenty of protection, Dietrich."

"Of course. I'll arrange it."

Belloq turned. The flight from Cairo was a lie, of course—he had already radioed instructions ahead to the island, without Dietrich's knowledge. It was a bridge he would cross when he reached it.

The only thing of any consequence now was that he should open the Ark before it was sent to Berlin.

There was wild confusion among the tents now. German soldiers had run to the airstrip and, in disarray, were returning. Another group of armed men, their faces darkened from the smoke of the ruin, had begun to load a canvas-covered truck with the Ark: Dietrich supervised them, shouting orders, his voice raised to a nervous pitch. He would be relieved and happy when this wretched crate was finally safe in Berlin, but meantime he didn't trust Belloq—he'd noticed some fierce light of purpose, a devious prupose, in the Frenchman's eyes. And behind this purpose something that looked manic, distant, as if the archaeologist had gone deeper into communing with himself. It was a look of madness, he thought, somewhat alarmed to realize he'd seen a similar look on the Führer's face when he'd been in Bavaria with Belloq. Maybe they were alike, this Frenchman and Adolf Hitler. Maybe their strength, as well as their madness, was what separated them from ordinary men. Dietrich could only guess. He stared at the crate going inside the truck now and he wondered about Jones—but Jones had to be dead, he had to be entombed in that dreadful chamber, surely. Even so, the Frenchman seemed convinced that the American had been behind the sabotage. Maybe this animosity, this rivalry, that existed between those two was yet another aspect of Belloq's lunacy.

Maybe.

There was no time to ruminate on the Frenchman's state of mind now. There was the Ark and the road to Cairo and the dread prospect of further sabotage along the way. Sweating, hating this dreary desert, this heat, he shouted once more at the men loading the truck—feeling somewhat sorry for them. Like himself, they were a long way from the Fatherland.

Marion and Indy had found their way behind some barrels, watching the Arabs run back and forth in confusion, watching the Germans load the truck. Their faces were blackened from the convulsions of the explosion and Marion, visibly pale even beneath the soot, had an appearance of extreme fatigue.

"You took your damn time," she complained.

"I got you out, didn't I?"

"At the last possible moment," she said. "How come you always leave things till then?"

He glanced at her, rubbed his fingertips in her face, stared at the soot imbedded in the whorls of his fingerprints, then he turned back to peer at the truck. "They're taking the Ark somewhere—which is what I'm more interested in right now."

A bunch of Arabs were running past now. Among them, to his pleasure and surprise, Indy saw Sallah.

He stuck out his foot, tripping the Egyptian, who tumbled over and got up again with a look of delight on his face.

"Indy! Marion! I thought I'd lost you."

"Likewise," Indy said. "What happened?"

"They barely pay the Arabs any attention, my friend. They assume we are fools, ignorant fools—besides, they can hardly tell one of us from the other. I slipped away and they weren't paying close attention in any case."

He slid behind the barrels, breathing hard.

"I assume you caused the explosion?"

"You got it."

"You don't know they are now planning to take the Ark in the truck to Cairo?"

"Cairo?"

"Presumably Berlin afterward."

"I doubt Berlin," Indy said. "I can't imagine Belloq allowing the Ark to reach Germany before he's dabbled with it."

An open staff car drew up alongside the truck. Belloq and Dietrich got inside with a driver and an armed guard. There was the sound of feet scuffling across the sand; ten or so armed soldiers climbed up into the rear of the truck with the Ark.

"It's hopeless," Marion said.

Indy didn't answer. Watch, he told himself. Watch and concentrate. *Think*. Now there was a second staff car, top open, with a machine-gun mounted in the back; a gunner sat restlessly behind it. In the front of this car Gobler was positioned behind the wheel. Alongside Gobler was Arnold Toht.

Marion drew her breath in sharply when she saw Toht. "He's a monster."

"They are all monsters," Sallah said.

"Monsters or not," she answered, "it looks more and more hopeless by the moment."

Machine gun, armed soldiers, Indy thought. Maybe something was possible. Maybe he didn't have to accept hopelessness as the only answer. He watched this convoy begin to pull out, swaying over the sands.

"I'm going to follow them," he said.

"How?" Marion asked. "You can run that fast?"

"I have a better idea." Indy got up. "You two get back to Cairo as fast as you can and arrange some kind of transportation to England—anything, a ship, a plane, I don't care."

"Why England?" Marion said.

"There are no language barriers and no Nazis," Indy said. He looked at Sallah. "Where can we meet in Cairo?"

Sallah looked thoughtful for a moment. "There is Omar's garage, where he keeps his truck. Do you know the Square of Snakes?"

"Gruesome," Indy said. "But I couldn't forget *that* address, could I?"

"In the Old City," Sallah said.

"I'll be there."

Marion stood up. "How do I know you'll get there in one piece?"

"Trust me."

He kissed her as she caught his arm. She said, "I wonder if a time will come when you'll stop leaving me?"

He skipped away, weaving between the barrels.

"We can use my truck," Sallah said to Marion after he'd gone. "Slow but safe."

Marion stared into space. What was it about Indy that so affected her, anyhow? He wasn't exactly a tender lover, if he could be called a lover of any kind. And he leaped in and out of her life in the manner of a jumping-bean. So what the devil was it? Some mysteries you just can't get to the bottom of, she thought. Some you don't even want to.

Indy had seen the stallions tethered to poles in a place between the abandoned airstrip and the excavations: two of them, a white Arabian and a black one, shaded from the sun by a strip of green canvas. Now, having left Marion and Sallah, he ran toward the stallions, hoping they'd still be there. They were. My lucky day, he thought.

He approached them cautiously. He hadn't ridden for years and he wondered if it was true that horseback riding, like bicycle riding, was something you never forgot once you'd learned it. He hoped so. The black stallion, snorting, pounding the sand with its hooves, reared up as he came near; the white horse, on the other hand, regarded him in a docile way. He heaved himself up on its white back, tugged at its mane, and felt it buck mildly, then move in the direction of his tugging. Go, he thought, and he rode the animal out of the canvas shelter, digging its sides with his heels. He galloped the animal, forcing it across the dunes, down gulleys, over ridges. It moved beautifully, responding to his gestures without complaint. He had to cut the convoy off somewhere along the mountainous roads between here and Cairo. After that—what the hell?

There was much to be said for spontaneity.

And the thrill of the chase.

The convoy struggled along a narrow mountain road that rose higher and higher, moving through hairpin turns that overlooked passes whose depths caused vertigo. Indy, astride the stallion, watched it go; it labored, grinding upward, some distance below him. And the guys in the trucks, uniformed zombies that they might be, still had rifles, and you had to respect, with great caution, any armed man. Especially when they were component parts of a small army and you—with more reckless courage than reason—were alone on an Arabian horse.

He urged the steed down a slope now, a slope of scrub and shale and soft soil, and its hooves created tiny avalanches. Then he hit the strip of road behind the rear staff car, once again hoping he wouldn't be seen. Fat chance, he thought.

He made the animal weave just as the gunner in the rear car opened fire, spraying the soft surface of the road with bullets that made the horse dance. The bullets echoed against the sides of the mountain. He drove the horse harder now, almost breaking the animal, and then he was passing the staff car, seeing the surprised faces of the Germans inside. The gunner swung his machine gun and it spluttered, kicked, running out of ammunition as he blasted futilely away at the man on the horse. Toht, seated beside the driver, pulled a pistol, but Indy was already obscured from the staff car by the truck, riding alongside the cab now. The German fired the pistol anyway. His shots ripped through the canvas of the truck.

Take your chance now, Indy thought. He jumped from the animal, spun through the air, caught the side of the cab and swung the door open as the armed guard riding with the driver tried to raise his rifle. Indy grappled with him for the weapon, twisting it this way and that while the guard grunted with the effort of a combat in which he didn't have the privilege of using his gun. Indy twisted hard; he heard the sudden sickening sound of wrists breaking, the cry of the man's pain, and then Indy forced the guard to drop from the cab out onto the road.

Now the driver.

Indy struggled with him, a stout man with gold teeth, as the steering wheel spun and the truck lunged toward the precipice. Indy reached for the wheel, pulling the truck back, and the driver struck him hard on the face.

Indy was stunned a moment. The driver tried to brake. Indy kicked his foot away. And then they were struggling together again as the wheel went into a purposeless spin and the truck swerved. In the staff car behind, Gobler had to swing his wheel to avoid the truck—a spin so sharp and so abrupt that the gunner in the rear was flipped from the side of the auto and over the edge of the cliff. He fell like a kite weighted with lead, arms outstretched and wind rushing through his hair, and the sound of his scream echoed in the canyon below.

In the lead staff car, Belloq turned to see what was going on. Jones, he thought: it had to be Jones, still trying to get the Ark. The prize will never be yours, friend, he thought. He stared at Dietrich, then he looked back once more, but sunlight obscured the view into the cab of the truck behind.

"I think there is a problem," Belloq said casually.

The car reached a summit, made a hairpin turn, struck the frail guardrail at the edge and bent it. The driver managed to get the car straight again, while the armed guard, seated in the rear of the car, leveled his submachine gun and trained it on the window of the cab.

Belloq restrained him: "If you shoot, you may kill the driver. If you kill the driver, your Führer's little Egyptian prize will very likely plummet over the side. What would I tell them in Berlin?"

Looking worried, Dietrich managed to nod in a grim way. "Is this more of your American friend's antics, Belloq?"

"What he hopes to achieve against such odds escapes me," Belloq said. "But it also scares me."

"If anything happens to the Ark . . ." Dietrich didn't finish his sentence, but he might have drawn an index finger, like a blade, across his larynx.

"Nothing will happen to the Ark," Belloq said.

Indy had his hands around the driver's neck now and the truck once again went out of control, spinning toward the broken guardrail, striking it flat, stirring up a cloud of dense dust before Indy caught the wheel and brought the truck back from the edge. In the staff car at the rear, the dust blinded Gobler and Toht—Toht, who was still holding his pistol in a useless manner.

Gobler, his throat thick from the dust, coughed. He tried to blink the dust out of his eyes. But he blinked too late. The last thing he saw was the broken guardrail, the last thing he heard the abrupt, fearful scream of Toht. The staff car, inexorably drawn to the edge of the pass as an iron filing to a magnet, went through the guardrail and dipped into space, seeming to hang for a second in some travesty of gravity before dropping, dropping and dropping, exploding in a wild burst of flame as it bounced down the side of the pass.

Damn, Indy thought. Whenever he tackled the driver, the truck almost carried them to certain death. And the guy was strong, the stoutness concealing a layer of muscle, hard muscle. From the corner of his eye, Indy was conscious of something else. He glanced at the side mirror—soldiers were clambering around the side of the truck, hanging on through fear and determination, making their way toward the cab. In one savage burst of strength, Indy shoved the driver away, slid the door open behind the wheel and kicked him out of the cab. The man bounced away in dust and screams, arms thrashing the air.

Sorry, Indy thought.

He seized the wheel and pressed the gas, gaining on the front staff car. Then there was a sudden darkness, a short tunnel cut into the side of the mountain. He swung the truck from side to side, scraping the walls of the tunnel, hearing the cries of the soldiers as they were smashed against walls, as they lost their grip on the side of the truck. Indy wondered how many other soldiers were still in the rear of his truck. Impossible to count. Out of the tunnel now, back in the hard daylight, he drove against the staff car, bumped it and watched the face of the armed guard as he looked upward, pointed—*he was pointing at the top of the truck.*

He's blown it, Indy thought. If there are more soldiers on the top of this truck, that guy has just blown the scheme. Better safe than sorry, he told himself, suddenly slamming on the brakes, locking the wheels, making the truck skid to a halt. He saw two soldiers thrown from the roof of the truck, shattered against the side of the mountain.

They were coming down from the high mountain road now. Indy put his foot on the gas, pressuring the staff car, bumping it; a good feeling, he thought, to know they won't take a chance on killing you because of your precious cargo. He enjoyed the sudden sensation of freedom, banging again and again at the rear bumper of the car, watching Belloq and his German friends being shaken, rattled. But he knew he'd have to get ahead of them sooner or later. Before Cairo, he'd have to be in front of them.

He thrust the truck forward again, hammering the staff car. The road was leveling out as it dropped from the mountain heights: in the far distance, dim as yet in outline, he could see the haze of the city. The dangerous part, the worst part now: if they ran no risk of watching him plunge the truck and its cargo down a steep pass, then they'd almost certainly try to kill him now, or at least run him off the road.

As if prompted by the thought, a form of treacherous telepathy, the armed guard opened fire. The bullets of the submachine gun shattered the glass, ripped through the canvas fabric, drove deep into the body of the truck. Indy heard them *zing* past him, but he ducked anyway, an instinctive thing. Now, for sure, he needed to get out in front. The road twisted still, going into a sharp bend just ahead. Hold on, he told himself. *Hold tight and make it here.* He gave the truck as much gas as he could and swung the vehicle around the staff car, hearing another whine of bullets, and then he was hitting the car and seeing it go off the road, where it slid down a short embankment.

One step completed. But he knew they'd get back on the road and come after him again. He glanced in his side mirror: yeah, sure enough. They were slithering back up from the incline, reversing across the road, straightening, coming after him. He shoved the gas pedal to the floor. Give me all you've got, he thought. And then he was on the outskirts of the city, the staff car immediately behind him. City streets: a different ball game.

Narrow thoroughfares. He drove quickly through them and sent animals and people flying, turning over stalls, baskets, the fruits of merchants and vendors, scattering beggars in his way. Pedestrians scurried into doorways when the truck wheeled through; then he was threading ever more narrow streets and alleys, looking for the square where Omar had his garage, replaying the geography of Cairo in his mind. A blind beggar suddenly capable of sight—a holy miracle—jumped out of the way, dropping his begging bowl and raising his dark glasses to peer at the truck.

He pushed the truck harder. The staff car still came on.

He swung the wheel. Another narrow alley. Donkeys jumped out of the path of the truck, a man fell from a stepladder, a baby in its mother's arms began to howl. Sorry, Indy thought. I'd stay and apologize in person, but I don't find it convenient right now.

Still he couldn't lose the staff car.

Then he was in the square. He saw the sign of Omar's garage, the door hanging wide open, and he drove the truck quickly through. The door was shut tight immediately as he brought the truck to a whining halt. Then several Arab boys with broomsticks and brushes began to erase the tracks of the vehicle while Indy, wondering if he'd made it, sat slumped behind the wheel in the darkness of the garage.

The staff car slowed, crossed the square and continued on its way, Belloq and Dietrich scrutinizing the streets with expressions of anguish and loss.

In the back of the truck, safe in the crate, the Ark began to hum almost inaudibly. It was as if within it, locked away and secure, a piece of machinery had spontaneously begun to operate. Nobody heard the sound.

It was dark when Sallah and Marion arrived at the garage. Indy had fallen asleep briefly in a cot Omar had provided, waking alone and hungry in the silent darkness. He rubbed his eyes when an overhead lamp was turned on. Marion had somewhere washed and brushed her hair and looked, well, Indy thought, *stunning*. She stood over him when he opened his eyes.

"You look pretty beat up," she said.

"A few surface cuts," he answered, sitting up, groaning, realizing that his body ached.

But then Sallah entered the room and Indy suddenly pushed aside his tiredness and his pain.

"We have a ship," Sallah said.

"Reliable?"

"The men are pirates, if I may use the phrase loosely. But you can trust them. Their captain, Katanga, is an honorable man—regardless of his more doubtful enterprises."

"They'll take us *and* the cargo?"

Sallah nodded. "For a price."

"What else?" Indy, stiff, got up. "Let's get this truck down to the harbor."

He gazed at Marion a moment, then he said, "I have a feeling that our day isn't quite finished yet."

In the ornate building that housed the German Embassy in Cairo, Dietrich and Belloq sat together in a room more commonly used by the Ambassador, a career diplomat who had survived the purges of Hitler and who, all too gladly, had vacated the room for their purposes. They had been sitting in silence for some time now, Belloq gazing at the portrait of Hitler, Dietrich restlessly smoking Egyptian cigarettes.

From time to time the telephone rang. Dietrich would answer it, replace it, then shake his head in Belloq's direction.

"If we have lost the Ark . . ." Dietrich lit another cigarette.

Belloq rose, walked around the room, waved a hand dismissively. "I will not countenance that prospect, Dietrich. What has happened to your wonderful Egyptian spy network? Why can't they find what your men so carelessly lost?"

"They will. I have every faith."

"Faith. I wish I had some of it myself."

Dietrich closed his eyes. He was weary of the sharp edge of Belloq's mood; and fearful, even more, of returning empty-handed to Berlin.

"I cannot believe such incompetence," Belloq said. "How could one man, acting alone—*alone*, remember—destroy most of a convoy *and* disappear into the bargain? Stupidity. I can hardly believe it."

"I've listened to this already," Dietrich said, annoyed.

Belloq walked to the window and stared out across the darkness. Somewhere, wrapped in this impenetrable Cairo night, was Jones; and Jones had the Ark. *Damn him.* The Ark could not be let go now; even the prospect caused him a chill, a sensation of something sinking inside him.

The telephone rang again. Dietrich picked it up, listened, and then his manner changed. When he hung up he looked at the Frenchman with a vague expression of vindication on his face. "I told you my network would turn something up."

"Did they?"

"According to a watchman at the docks, an Egyptian named Sallah, the friend of Jones, chartered a merchant steamer by the name of the *Bantu Wind.*"

"It may be a ruse," Belloq said.

"It may be. But it's worth looking into."

"We don't have anything else anyhow," Belloq said.

"Then shall we go?"

They left the Embassy hurriedly, reaching the docks only to discover that the tramp steamer had sailed an hour ago. Its destination was unknown.

11: The Mediterranean

In the captain's cabin of the *Bantu Wind*, Indy stripped to the waist, and Marion dressed his assorted cuts and wounds with bandages and a bottle of iodine. He stared at her as she worked, noticing the dress she'd changed into. It was white, high-necked, somewhat prim. He found it appealing in its way.

"Where did you get that, anyhow?" he asked.

"There's a whole wardrobe in the closet," she said. "I get the feeling I'm not the first woman to travel with these pirates."

"I like it," he said.

"I feel like a—*ahem*—a virgin."

"I guess you look like one."

She regarded him a moment, pressing iodine to a cut. Then she said, "Virginity is one of those elusive things, honey. When it's gone, it's gone. Your account is well and truly spent."

She stopped working on him, sat down, poured herself a small glass of rum from a bottle. She sipped it, watching him as she did so, seeming to tease him over the rim of the glass.

"Did I ever apologize for burning down your tavern?" he said.

"I can't say you did. Did I ever thank you for getting me out of that burning plane?"

He shook his head. "We're even. Maybe we should consider the past closed, huh?"

She was silent for a long time.

"Where does it hurt?" she asked tenderly.

"Everywhere."

Marion softly kissed his left shoulder. "Here?"

Indy jumped a little in response. "Yes, there."

Marion leaned closer to him. "Where *doesn't* it hurt?" And she kissed his elbow. "Here?"

He nodded. She kissed the top of his head. Then he pointed to his neck and she kissed him there. Then the tip of his nose, his eyes. Then he touched his own lips and she kissed him, her mouth gently devouring his.

She was different; she had changed. This was no longer the wild touch he'd encountered in Nepal.

Something had touched her, softened her.

He wondered what it had been.

He wondered at the change.

The crated Ark lay in the hold of the ship. Its presence agitated the ship's rats: they scurried back and forward pointlessly, trembling, whiskers shivering. Still silent as a whisper, the same faint humming sound emerged from the crate. Only the rats, their hearing hypersensitive, picked up on the sound; and it obviously scared them.

On the bridge, as the first light of dawn streaked the ocean, Captain Katanga smoked a pipe and watched the surface of the water as if he were trying to discern something that would have been invisible to landlocked men. He let the sun and the salt spray play against his face, streaks of salt leaving white crystalline traces on his black skin. There was something out there, something emerging from the dark, but he wasn't sure what. He narrowed his eyes, stared, saw nothing. He listened to the faintly comforting rattle of the ship's weary engines and thought of a failing heart trying to pump blood through an old body. He considered Indy and the woman a moment. He liked them both, and besides, they were friends of Sallah's.

But something about the cargo, something about the crate, made him uneasy. He wasn't sure what; he only knew he'd be glad to get rid of it when the time came. It was the same unease he experienced now as his eyes scanned the ocean. A vague pulse. A thing you just couldn't put your finger on. But there was something out there just the same, something moving. He knew it even if he couldn't see it.

He smelled, as certainly as the salt flecks in the air, the distinctive odor of danger.

He continued to watch, his body poised in the manner of a man about to jump from a high diving board. A man who cannot swim.

When Indy woke, he watched Marion for a time. She was still asleep, still looking virginal in the white dress. She had her face tilted to one side, and her mouth was slightly open. He rubbed at his bandages where his skin had begun to itch. Sallah had had the foresight to fetch his clothes, so he changed into his shirt now, made sure the bullwhip was secure at his back, then put on the leather jacket and played with the rim of the battered felt hat.

A lucky hat, he thought sometimes. Without it, he would have felt naked.

Marion turned over, her eyes opening.

"What a pleasant sight," she said.

"I don't feel pleasant," he answered.

She stared at his bandages and asked, "Why do you always get yourself into such scrapes?"

She sat up, stroking her hair, looking round the cabin. "I'm glad to see you changed clothes. You weren't convincing as an Arab, I'm afraid."

"I did my best."

She yawned and stretched and rose from the cot. He thought there was something delightful in the movement, a quality that touched him—touched him obliquely, in an off-center way. She reached for his hand, kissed the back of it, then moved around the cabin.

"How long are we going to be at sea?" she asked.

"Is that a literal or a metaphorical question?"

"Take it any way you like, Jones."

He smiled at her.

And then he understood that something had happened: while he'd been so involved in the act of introspection, the ship's engines had stopped and the vessel was no longer moving.

He rose and rushed to the door, clambering onto the deck and then the bridge, where Katanga was staring across the ocean. The captain's pipe was unlit, his face solemn.

"You appear to have some important friends, Mr. Jones," the man said.

Indy stared. At first he couldn't make anything out. But then, following the sweep of the captain's hand, he saw that the *Bantu Wind*, like a spinster courted by an unwanted entourage of voracious suitors, was surrounded by about a dozen German Wolf submarines.

"Holy shit," he said.

"My sentiments exactly," Katanga said. "You and the girl must disappear quickly. We have a place in the hold for you. But quickly! Get the girl!"

It was too late: both men noticed five rafts, with armed boarding parties, circle the steamer. Already the first Nazis were climbing the rope ladders that had been dropped. He turned, ran. Marion was uppermost in his mind now. He had to get her first. Too late—the air was filled with the sound of boots, German accents, commands. Ahead of him he saw Marion being dragged from the cabin by a couple of soldiers. The rest of the soldiers, boarding quickly, rounded the crew on deck, guns trained on them. Indy melted into the shadows, slipping through a doorway into the labyrinth of the ship.

Before he vanished, his brain working desperately for a way out, he heard Marion curse her assailants; and despite the situation, he smiled at her spirit. A good woman, he thought, and impossible to subdue entirely. He liked her for that.

He liked her a lot.

Dietrich came on board, followed by Belloq. The captain had already given his crew a signal not to resist the invaders. The men clearly wanted to fight, but the odds were against them. So they lined up sullenly under the German guns as Belloq and Dietrich strode past, shouting orders, sending soldiers scampering all over the ship for the Ark.

Marion watched as Belloq approached her. She felt something of the same vibrations as before, but this time she was determined to fight them, determined not to yield to whatever sensations the man might arouse in her.

"My dear," Belloq said. "You must regale me with the tale—no doubt epic—of how you managed to escape from the Well. It can wait until later, though."

Marion said nothing. Was there no end in sight to this whole sequence of affairs? Indy apparently had a marvelous talent for dragging wholesale destruction behind him. She watched Belloq, who touched her lightly under the chin. She pulled her face away. He smiled.

"Later," he said, passing on to where Katanga stood.

He was about to say something when a sound seized his attention and he turned, noticing a group of soldiers raise the crated Ark from the hold. He fought the impatience he felt. The world, with all its mundane details, always intruded on his ambition. But that was going to be over soon. Slowly, reluctantly, he took his eyes from the crate as Dietrich gave the order for it to be placed aboard one of the submarines.

He looked at Katanga. "Where is Jones?"

"Dead."

"Dead?" Belloq said.

"What good was he to us? We killed him. We threw him overboard. The girl has more value in the kind of marketplace in which I dabble. A man like Jones is useless to me. If his cargo was what you wanted, I only ask that you take it and leave us with the girl. It will reduce our loss on this trip."

"You make me impatient," Belloq said. "You expect me to believe Jones is dead?"

"Believe what you wish. I only ask that we proceed in peace."

Dietrich had approached now. "You are in no position to ask anything, Captain. We will decide what we wish to decide, and then we must consider the question of whether we will blow this ancient ship out of the water."

"The girl goes with me," Belloq said.

Dietrich shook his head.

Belloq continued: "Consider her part of my compensation. I'm sure the Führer would approve. Given that we have obtained the Ark, Dietrich."

Dietrich appeared hesitant.

"If she fails to please me, of course, you may throw her to the sharks, for all I care."

"Very well," Dietrich said. He noticed a brief expression of doubt on Belloq's face, then signaled for Marion to be taken aboard the submarine.

Indy watched from his hiding place in an air ventilator, his body hunched and uncomfortable. Boots scraped the deck unpleasantly close to his face—but he hadn't been discovered. Katanga's lie seemed feeble to him, a desperate gesture if a kind one. But it had worked. He peered along the deck, thinking. He had to go with the submarine, he had to go with Marion, with the Ark. How? Exactly how?

Belloq was watching the captain closely. "How do I know you are telling the truth about Jones?"

Katanga shrugged. "I don't lie." He stared at the Frenchman; this one he didn't like at all. He felt sorry for Indy for having an enemy like Belloq.

"Have your people found him on board?" the seaman asked.

Belloq considered this; Dietrich shook his head.

The German said, "Let us leave. We have the Ark. Alive or dead, Jones is of no importance now."

Belloq's face and his body went tense a moment; then he appeared to relax, following Dietrich from the deck of the tramp steamer.

Indy could hear the rafts leaving the sides of the *Bantu Wind*. Then he moved quickly, emerging from his place of concealment and running along the deck.

Aboard the submarine Belloq entered the communications room. He placed earphones on his head, picked up the microphone and uttered a call signal. After a time he heard a voice broken by static. The accent was German.

"Captain Mohler. This is Belloq."

The voice was very faint, distant. "Everything has been prepared in accordance with your last communication, Belloq."

"Excellent." Belloq took the headphones off. Then he left the radio room, walking toward the small forward cabin, where the woman was being held. He stepped inside the room. She sat on a bunk, her expression glum. She didn't look up as he approached her. He reached out, touched her lightly under the chin, raised her face.

"You have nice eyes," he said. "You shouldn't hide them."

She twisted her face to the side.

He smiled. "I imagined we might continue our unfinished business."

She got up from the bunk, went across the room. "We don't *have* any unfinished business."

"I think we do." He reached out and tried to hold her hand; she jerked her arm free of him. "You resist? You didn't resist before, my dear. Why the change of heart?"

"Things are a little different," she answered.

He regarded her in silence for a time. Then he said, "You feel something for Jones? Is that it?"

She looked away, staring vacantly across the room.

"Poor Jones," Belloq said. "I fear he's destined never to win anything."

"What is that supposed to mean?"

Belloq went toward the door. There, on his way out, he turned around. "You don't even know, my dear, if he's alive or dead. Do you?"

Then he closed the door and moved into the narrow passageway. Several seamen walked past him. They were followed by Dietrich, whose face was angry, stern. It amused Belloq to see this look: in his anger, Dietrich looked preposterous, like an enraged schoolmaster powerless to punish a recalcitrant pupil.

"Perhaps you would be good enough to explain yourself, Belloq."

"What is there to explain?"

Dietrich seemed to be struggling with an urge to strike the Frenchman. "You have given specific orders to the captain of this vessel to proceed to a certain supply base—an island located off the African coast. It was my understanding that we would return to Cairo and then fly the Ark to Berlin on the first available flight. Why have you taken the liberty of changing the plan, Belloq? Are you suddenly under the impression that you are an admiral in the German navy? Is that it? Have your delusions of grandeur gone that far?"

"Delusions of grandeur," Belloq said, still amused by Dietrich. "I hardly think so, Dietrich. My point is that we open the Ark before taking it to Berlin. Would you be comfortable, my friend, if your Führer found the Ark to be empty? Don't you want to be sure that the Ark contains sacred relics *before* we return to Germany? I am trying to imagine the awful disappointment on Adolf's face if he finds nothing inside the Ark."

Dietrich stared at the Frenchman; his anger had passed, replaced by a look of doubt, incredulity. "I don't trust you, Belloq. I have never trusted you."

"Thank you."

Dietrich paused before going on: "I find it curious that you want to open the Ark on some obscure island instead of taking the more convenient route—

namely Cairo. Why can't you look inside your blessed box in Egypt, Belloq?"

"It wouldn't be fitting," Belloq said.

"Can you explain that?"

"I could—but you would not understand, I fear."

Dietrich looked angry; he felt his authority once more had been undermined—but the Frenchman had the Führer as an ally. What could he do, faced with that fact?

He turned quickly and walked away. Belloq watched him go. For a long time the Frenchman didn't move. He felt a great sense of anticipation all at once, thinking of the island. The Ark could have been opened almost anywhere—in that sense Dietrich was correct. But it was appropriate, Belloq thought, that it should be opened on the island. It should be opened in a place whose atmosphere was heavy with the distant past, a place of some historic importance. Yes, Belloq thought. The setting had to match the moment. There had to be a correspondence between the Ark and its environment. Nothing else would do.

He went to the small supply cabin where the crate lay.

He looked at it for a while, his mind empty. What secrets? What can you tell me? He reached out and touched the crate. Did he simply imagine he felt a vibration from the box? Did he simply imagine he heard a faint sound? He closed his eyes, his hand still resting on the wooden surface. A moment of intense awe: he could see some great void, a sublime darkness, a boundary he would step across into a place beyond language and time. He opened his eyes; the tips of his fingers tingled.

Soon, he said to himself.

Soon.

The sea was cold, swirling around him in small whirlpools created by the submarine's motions. Indy hung to the rail, his muscles aching, the wet whip contracting in water and clinging, too tightly, to his body. You could drown, he thought, and he tried to remember whether drowning was said to be a good way to go. It might arguably be better than hanging to the rail of the submarine that could plunge abruptly into the depths. At any moment, too. He wondered if heroes could apply for retirement benefits. He hauled himself up, swinging his body onto the deck. Then it struck him.

His hat. His hat had gone.

Don't be superstitious now. You don't have time to mourn the passing of a lucky hat.

The sub began to submerge. Perceptibly, it was sinking like a huge metallic fish. He rushed across the deck, water at his waist now. He reached the conning tower, then began to climb the ladder. At the top of the turret he looked down: the sub was still sinking. Water was rushing, wildly swirling foam, toward him. The turret was being consumed by the rising water, and then the radio mast was sinking too. He moved, treading water, to the periscope. He hung on to it as the vessel continued to sink. If it went under entirely, then he was lost. The periscope started to go down, too. Down and down, while he gripped it. Please, he thought, please don't go down any further. But this is what comes of trying to stow yourself away on a German submarine. You can't expect the old red-carpet treatment, can you?

Freezing, shivering, he hung on to the periscope; and then, as if some merciful divinity of the ocean had heard his unspoken prayers, the vessel stopped its dive. It left only three feet of the periscope out of water. But three feet was something to be thankful for. Three feet was all he needed to survive. *Don't sink any deeper,* he thought. Then he realized he was talking aloud, not thinking. It might have been, in other circumstances, funny—trying to hold a rational conversation with several tons of good German metal. *I'm out of my mind. That's what it is. And all this is just hallucination. A nautical madness.*

Indy took the bullwhip and lashed himself to the periscope, hoping that if he fell asleep he wouldn't wake to find himself on the black ocean bottom, or worse—food for the fishes.

The cold seeped through him. He tried to stop his teeth from knocking together. And the bullwhip, heavy with water, was cutting into his skin. He tried to remain alert, prepared for whatever contingency might arise—but weariness was a weight in him now, and sleep seemed the most promising prospect of all.

He shut his eyes. He tried to think of something, anything, that would keep him from dropping off—but it was hard. He wondered where the submarine was headed. He sang little songs in his head. He tried to remember all the telephone numbers he'd ever known. He wondered about a girl named Rita he'd almost married once: where was she now? A lucky escape there, he thought.

But he was weary and the thoughts circled aimlessly.

And he drifted off into sleep, despite the cold, despite his discomfort. He drifted away, the sleep dreamless and dead.

When he woke it was daylight and he wasn't sure how long he'd slept, whether he'd slept a whole day away. He could no longer feel his body: total numbness. And his skin was puckered from the water, fingertips soft and wrinkled. He adjusted the bullwhip and looked around. There was a land mass ahead, an island, a semitropical place—halcyon, he thought. He stared at the rich foliage. Green, wonderful and deep and restful. The submarine approached the island, skimming into what looked like a cave. Inside, the Germans had built a complete underground supply base and submarine pen. *And there were more uniformed Nazis on this dock than you could have found in one of Hitler's Nuremberg extravaganzas.*

How could he fail to be seen?

He quickly drew himself clear of his whip, and he slipped into the water. He submerged, realizing he'd left his whip attached to the scope. The whip and the hat: it was a day for sad farewells to treasured possessions, for sure.

He swam toward the island, trying to remain underwater as much as he could. He saw the sub rise as it went toward the dock. Then he was stumbling onto the beach, glad to feel earth under him again, even if it was the earth of some Nazi paradise. He made his way over the sand to a high point where he had a good view of the dock. The crate was lifted from the sub, supervised by Belloq, who appeared to live in anxious expectation of somebody's dropping his precious relic. He hovered around the crate like a surgeon over a dying patient.

And then there was Marion, surrounded by a bunch of uniformed fools who were pushing her forward.

He sat down in the sand, hidden by rushes that grew on the edge of the dunes.

Inspiration, he thought. That's what I need now.

In a good-sized dose.

12: **A Mediterranean Island**

It was late afternoon when Belloq met Mohler. He was not entirely happy with the idea of Dietrich's being involved in the conversation. The damned man was certain to ask questions, and his impatience had already begun to make Belloq nervous, as though it were contagious.

Captain Mohler said, "Everything has been prepared in accordance with your instructions, Belloq."

"Nothing has been overlooked?"

"Nothing."

"Then the Ark must be taken to that place now."

Mohler glanced a moment at Dietrich. Then he turned and began to supervise a group of soldiers while they placed the crate in a jeep.

Dietrich, who had been silent, was annoyed. "What does he mean? What preparations are you talking about?"

"It need not concern you, Dietrich."

"Everything connected with this accursed Ark concerns me."

"I am going to open the Ark," Belloq said. "However, there are certain . . . certain preconditions connected with the act."

"Preconditions? Such as?"

"I don't think you should worry, my friend. I don't want to be the one responsible for overloading your already much-worked brain."

"You can spare me the sarcasm, Belloq. Sometimes it seems to me that you forget who is in charge here."

Belloq stared at the crate for a time. "You must understand—it is not simply the act of opening a box, Dietrich. There is a certain amount of ritual involved. We are not exactly dealing with a box of hand grenades, you understand. This is not any ordinary undertaking."

"What ritual?"

"You will see in good time, Dietrich. However, it need not alarm you."

"If anything happens to the Ark, Belloq, *anything*, I will personally pull the hanging rope on your scaffold. Do you understand me?"

Belloq nodded. "Your concern for the Ark is touching. But you needn't worry. It will be safe and delivered to Berlin finally, and your Führer can add another relic to his lovely collection. Yes?"

"You better be as good as your word."

"I will be. I will be."

Belloq looked at the crated Ark before staring into the jungle beyond the dock area. It lay in there, the place where the Ark would be opened.

"The girl," Dietrich said. "I also hate loose ends. What do we do with the girl?"

"I take it I can leave that to your discretion," Belloq said. "She is of no consequence to me."

Nothing is, he thought: nothing is of any consequence now, except for the Ark. Why had he bothered to entertain any kind of sentiment for the girl? Why had he even remotely troubled himself with the idea of protecting her? Human feelings were worthless compared to the Ark. All human experience faded into nothing. If she lived or died, what did it matter?

He experienced the same delicious sense of anticipation as before: it was hard, damnably hard, to take his eyes from the crate. It lay in the back of a jeep, magnetizing him. I will know your secrets, he thought. I will know all your secrets.

Indy skirted the trees at the edge of the dock area. He watched Marion, flanked by her Nazi escorts, get inside a jeep. The jeep was then driven off into the jungle. Belloq and the German climbed into another jeep and, moving steadily behind the vehicle that held the Ark, went off in the same direction as Marion. Where the hell are they going? Indy wondered. He began to move silently through the trees.

The German appeared in front of him, a materialization looming over him. He reached for his holster, but before he could get his pistol out, Indy picked up the branch of a tree, a slab of rotted wood, and struck him hard across the throat. The German, a young man, put his fingers to his larynx as if surprised, and blood began to spill from his mouth. His eyes rolled backward in his head, then he slipped to his knees. Indy hit him a second time across the skull, and he toppled over. What do you do with an unconscious Nazi? he wondered.

He stared at the man for a time before the notion came to him.

Why not?

Why not indeed?

The jeep that carried Belloq and Dietrich moved slowly through a canyon.

Dietrich said, "I am unhappy with this ritual."

You will be even more unhappy soon, Belloq thought. The trappings of what you so trivially call a ritual will cause a knot in your wooden brain, my friend.

"Is it essential?"

"Yes," Belloq said.

Dietrich just stared at the crate in the jeep ahead.

"It may console you to consider the prospect that by tomorrow the Ark will be in your Führer's hands."

Dietrich sighed.

The Frenchman was insane, he was convinced of

this. Somewhere along the way the Ark had warped whatever judgment he might have had. You could see it in his eyes, hear it in the clipped way of talking he seemed to have developed in recent days, and you could sense it in the oddly nervous gestures he continued to make.

Dietrich wouldn't be happy until he was back, mission complete, in Berlin.

The jeep came out into a clearing now, a clearing filled with tents and camouflaged shelters, barracks, vehicles, radio masts; a swarm of activity, soldiers rushing everywhere. Dietrich surveyed the depot proudly, but Belloq was oblivious to it all. The Frenchman was staring beyond the clearing to a stone outcropping on the other side—a pinnacle some thirty feet high with a flat slab at the top. Into the sides of the slope some ancient tribe, some lost species, had carved primitive steps. The appearance was like an altar—and it was this fact that had brought Belloq here. An altar, a natural arrangement of rock that might have been designed by God for the very purpose of opening the Ark.

He couldn't speak for a time. He stared at the rock until Captain Mohler came and tapped him on the shoulder.

"Do you wish to prepare now?" the German asked.

Belloq nodded. He followed the German to a tent. He was thinking of the lost tribe that had cut those steps, that had left its own relics scattered here and there, in the form of broken statues suggesting forgotten divinities, across the island. The religious connotations of the place were exactly right: the Ark had found a place that matched its own splendor. It was correct: nowhere else could have been better.

"The white silk tent," Belloq said. He touched the soft material.

"As you ordered," Mohler said.

"Fine, fine." And Belloq stepped inside. A chest sat in the middle of the floor. He opened the lid and looked inside. The ceremonial robe was elaborately embroidered. In wonder, he leaned forward to touch it. Then he looked at the German.

"You've followed my orders thoroughly. I am pleased."

The German had something in his hand: an ivory rod about five feet in length. He passed it to Belloq, who fingered the inlaid carvings of the piece.

"Perfect," Belloq said. "The Ark has to be opened, in accordance with sacred rites, with an ivory rod. And the one who opens the Ark must wear these robes. You did very well."

The German smiled. "You will not forget our little arrangement."

"I promise," Belloq said. "When I return to Berlin I will personally speak to the Führer about you in the highest possible terms."

"Thank you."

"Thank *you*," Belloq said.

The German regarded the robes a moment. "They suggest a certain Jewishness, don't they?"

"They should, my friend. They are Jewish."

"You will make yourself very popular around here with those things on."

"I am not interested in a popularity contest, Mohler."

Mohler watched as Belloq slipped the robes over his head, watched as the ornate brocade fell all around him. It was a total transformation: the man had even begun to look holy. Well, Mohler thought, it takes all sorts. Besides, even if he were mad, Belloq still had access to Hitler—and that was all that mattered.

"Is it dark outside?" Belloq asked. He felt peculiar, distanced from himself, as if his identity had begun to disintegrate and he'd become a stranger in a body that was only vaguely familiar.

"Soon," the German said.

"We must start at sunset. It's important."

"They have carried the Ark to the slab, as you wanted, Belloq."

"Good." He touched the robes, the upraised stitches

in the material. Belloq—even his name seemed strange to him. It was as if something spiritual, immaterial, had begun to consume him. He was floating outside of himself, it seemed—a perception that had the intensity, as well as the vagueness, of a narcotic response.

He picked up the ivory rod and stepped outside of the tent.

Almost everywhere, the German soldiers stopped in their activities and turned to look at him. He faintly understood the vibrations of repulsion, the animosity directed to his robes. But once again this notion reached him across some great distance. Dietrich was walking at his side, saying something. And Belloq had to concentrate hard to understand.

"A *Jewish* ritual? Are you crazy, man?"

Belloq said nothing. He moved toward the foot of the ancient steps; the sun, an outrage of color as it waned, hung low in the distance, touching everything with a bewildering array of oranges and reds and yellows.

He moved to the first step, glancing briefly at the German soldiers around him. Klieg lights had been set up, illuminating the stairs, the Ark. Belloq was certain, as he looked at it, that he heard it humming. And he was almost sure that it began to emit a glow of some kind. But then something happened, something distracted him, pulled him back to earth; a movement, a shadow, he couldn't be sure. He swung around to see one of the soldiers behave in a strange fashion, moving in a hunched way. He wore his helmet at an awkward angle, as if he sought to conceal his face. But it wasn't just this that so distracted Belloq, it was a weird sense of familiarity.

What? How? He stared—realizing that the soldier was struggling under the weight of a grenade launcher, which he hadn't noticed at first in the dying light. But that strange sense, that itch—what did it mean? A darkness crossed his mind. A darkness that was lit only when the soldier removed his helmet and leveled the grenade launcher up the steps at the Ark—the

Ark, which had been de-crated and looked vulnerable up on the slab.

"Hold it," Indy shouted. "One move from anybody and I blow that box back to Moses."

"Jones, your persistence surprises me. You are going to give mercenaries a bad name," Belloq said.

Dietrich interrupted. "Dr. Jones, surely you don't think you can escape from this island."

"That depends on how reasonable we're all willing to be. All I want is the girl. We'll keep possession of the Ark only until we've got safe transport to England. Then it's all yours."

"If we refuse?" Dietrich wanted to know.

"Then the Ark and some of us are going up in a big bang. And I don't think Hitler would like that a bit."

Indy began to move toward Marion, who was struggling with her bonds.

"You look fine in a German outfit, Jones," Belloq said.

"You look pretty good in your robes too."

But somebody else was moving now, approaching Indy from behind. And even as the girl began to scream in warning, Belloq recognized Mohler. The captain threw himself at Indy, knocking the weapon from his hand and bringing him to the ground. Jones —a gallant heart, Belloq thought, a reckless courage —lashed out at the soldier with his fist, then drove his knee upward in Mohler's groin. The captain groaned and rolled away, but Indy was already surrounded by soldiers, and although he fought them, although he fell kicking amid a bunch of helmets and jackboots, he was overpowered by numbers. Belloq shook his head and smiled in a pale way. He looked at Indy, who was being pinned by soldiers.

"A good try, Jones. A good effort."

And then Dietrich was coming through the ranks. "Foolish, very foolish," he said. "I cannot believe your recklessness."

"I'm trying to give it up," Indy said. He struggled with the soldiers who held him: useless.

"I have the cure for it," Dietrich said. He took his pistol from its holster, smiling.

Indy stared at the gun, then glanced at Marion, who had her eyes shut tight and was sobbing in a broken way.

Dietrich raised the pistol, aimed.

"Wait!"

Belloq's voice was thunderous, awesome, and his face looked malign in the intense light of the klieg lamps. The gun in Dietrich's hand was lowered.

Belloq said, "This man has been an irritation to me for years, Colonel Dietrich. Sometimes, I admit, he has amused me. And although I would also like to witness his end, I would like him to suffer one last defeat. Let him live until I have opened the Ark. Let him live that long. Whatever treasures may lie in the Ark will be denied him. The contents will be hidden from his view. I enjoy the idea. This is a prize he has dreamed of for years—and now he will never get any closer to it. When I have opened the Ark, you can dispose of him. For now, I suggest you tie him up beside the girl." And Belloq laughed, a hollow laugh that echoed in the darkness.

Indy was dragged to the statue and bound against it, his shoulder to Marion's.

"I'm afraid, Indy," she said.

"There's never been a better time for it."

The Ark began to hum, and Indy turned to watch Belloq climb the steps to the altar. It galled him to think of Belloq's hands on the Ark, Belloq opening it. *The prize.* And he would see none of it. You live a lifetime with the constant ambition of reaching a goal, and then, when it's there, when it's in front of you, *wham*—all you have left is the bitter taste of defeat. How could he watch the insane Frenchman, dressed like some medieval rabbi, go up the steps to the Ark?

How could he *not* watch?

"I think we're going to die, Indy," Marion said. "Unless you've figured something out."

Indy, barely hearing her, said nothing: there was something else now, something that was beginning to intrude on his mind—the sound of humming, low and constant, that seemed to be emerging from the Ark. How could that be? He stared at Belloq as the robed figure climbed to the slab.

"So how do we get out of this?" Marion asked again.

"God knows."

"Is that a play on words?" she said.

"Maybe."

"It's a hell of a time to be making bad jokes, Jones." She turned to him; there were circles of fatigue under her eyes. "Still. I love you for it."

"Do you?"

"Love you? Sure."

"I think it's reciprocal," Indy said, a little surprised at himself.

"It's also somewhat doomed," Marion said.

"We'll see."

Belloq, remembering the words of an old Hebraic chant, words he'd remembered from the parchment that had had the picture of the headpiece, started to sing in a low, monotonous way. He chanted as he climbed the steps, hearing the sound of the Ark accompany his voice, the sound of humming. It was growing in intensity, rumbling, filling the darkness. The Ark's power, the Ark's intense power. It moved in Belloq's blood, bewildering, demanding to be understood. The power. The knowledge. He paused near the top of the steps, chanting still but unable to hear his own voice now. The humming, the humming—it was growing, slicing through the night, filling all the silences. Then he climbed more, reached the top, stared at the Ark. Despite the dust of centuries, despite neglect, it was the most beautiful thing Belloq had ever seen. And it glowed, it glowed, feebly at first and then more brightly, as he looked at it. He was filled with wonder, watching the angels, the shining gold, the inner glow. The noise, too, rumbled through him, shook and surprised him. He felt himself begin to vibrate, as if the tremor might cause him to disintegrate and go spinning out into space. But there wasn't space, there wasn't time: his entire being was defined by the Ark, delineated by this relic of man's communication with God.

Speak to me.

Tell me what you know, tell me what the secrets of existence are.

His own voice seemed to be issuing from every part of his body now, through mouth, pores, blood cells. And he was rising, floating, distinct from the rigid world of logic all around him, defying the laws of the universe. *Speak to me. Tell me.* He raised the ivory rod, placing it under the lid, then labored to pry the lid open. The humming was louder now, all-consuming. He didn't hear the klieg lights explode below, the showers of broken glass that fell like worthless diamonds into the darkness. The humming—the voice of God, he thought. *Speak to me. Speak to me.* And then, as he worked with the rod, he felt suddenly blank, as if he hadn't existed until this moment, as if all memories had been erased, blank and strangely calm, at peace, undergoing a sense of oneness with the night around him, linked by all kinds of connections to the universe. Bound to the cosmos, to all matter that floated and expanded and shrank in the farthest estuaries of space, to exploding stars, spinning planets, and even to the unknowable dark of infinity. He ceased to exist. Whoever Belloq had been, he was no longer. He was nothing now: he existed only as the sound that came from the Ark. The sound of God.

"He's going to open it," Indy said.

"The noise," Marion said. "I wish I could put my hands to my ears. What is that noise?"

"The Ark."

"The Ark?"

Indy was thinking about something, an eclipsed memory, something that shifted loosely in his mind. What? What was it? Something he'd heard recently.

What? The Ark. Something to do with the Ark. *What what what?*

The Ark, the Ark—try to remember!

Up on the slab, at the top of the crude steps, Belloq was trying to open the lid. Lamps were exploding in violent showers of sharded glass. Even the moon, visible now in the night sky, seemed like an orb about to erupt and shatter. The night, the whole night, was like a great bomb attached to the end of a short fuse —a lit fuse, Indy thought. What is it? What am I trying to remember?

The lid was opening.

Belloq, sweating, perspiring in the heavy robes, applied the ivory rod while he kept up the chant that was inaudible now under the noise of the Ark. The moment. The moment of truth. Revelation. The mysterious networks of the divine. He groaned and raised the lid. It sprung open all at once and the light that emanated from within blinded him. But he didn't step away, didn't step back, didn't move. The light hypnotized him as surely as the sound mesmerized him. He was devoid of the capacity to move. Muscles froze. His body ceased to work. *The lid.*

It was the last thing he saw.

Because then the night was filled with fire rockets that screamed out of the Ark, pillars of flame that stunned the darkness, outreaches of fire searing the heavens. A white circle of light made a flashing ring around the island, a light that made the ocean glow and whipped up currents of spray, forcing a broken tide to rise upward in the dark. *The light, it was the light of the first day of the universe, the light of newness, of things freshly born, it was the light that God made: the light of creation.* And it pierced Belloq with the hard brightness of an inconceivable diamond, a light beyond the sorrowful limitations of any precious stone. It carved at his heart, shattered him. And it was more than a light—it was a weapon, a force, that drove through Belloq and lit him with the power of a billion candles: he was white, orange, blue, savaged by this electricity that stormed from the Ark.

And he smiled.

He smiled because, for a moment, he *was* the power. The power absorbed him. There was no distinction between the man and the force. Then the moment passed. Then his eyes disintegrated in the sockets, leaving black sightless holes, and his skin began to peel from the bone, curling back as if seized by a sudden leprosy, rotting, burning, scorched, blackened. And still he smiled. He smiled even as he began to change from something human to something touched by God, touched by God's rage, something that turned, silently, to a layer of dust.

When the lights began to shaft the dark, when the entire sky was filling with the force of the Ark, Indy had involuntarily shut his eyes—blinded by the power. And then all at once he remembered, he remembered what had eluded him before, the night he'd spent in the house of Imam: *Those who would open the Ark and release its force will die if they look upon it . . .* And through the noise, the blinding white pillars that had made the stars fade, he'd called to Marion: *Don't look!*

Keep your eyes closed!

She had twisted her face away from the first flare, the eruption of fire, and then, even if what he said puzzled her, she shut her eyes tight. She was afraid, afraid and overawed. And still she wanted to look. Still she was drawn to the great celestial flare, to the insane destruction of the night.

Don't look—he kept saying that even as she felt herself weaken.

He kept repeating it. Screaming it.

The night, like a dynamo, hummed, groaned, roared; the lights that seared the night seemed to howl.

Don't look don't look don't look!

The upraised tower of flame devastated. It hung in the sky like the shadow of a deity, a burning, shifting shadow composed not of darkness but of light, pure light. It hung there, both beautiful and monstrous, and it blinded those who looked upon it. It ripped eyes from the faces of the soldiers. It turned them from men into uniformed skeletons, covering the ground with bones, the black marks of scorches, covering everything with human debris. It burned the island, flattened trees, overturned boats, smashed the dock itself. It changed everything. Fire and light. It destroyed as though it were an anger that might never be appeased.

It broke the statue to which Indy and Marion were tied: the statue crumbled until it ceased to exist. And then the lid of the Ark slammed shut on the slab and the night became dark again and the ocean was silent. Indy waited for a long time before he looked.

The Ark was shining up there.

Shining with an intensity that suggested a contented silence; and a warning, a warning filled with menace.

Indy stared at Marion.

She was looking around speechlessly, staring at what the Ark had created. Wreckage, ruin, death. She opened her mouth, but she didn't speak.

There was nothing to say.

Nothing.

The earth around them hadn't been scorched. It was untouched.

She raised her face to the Ark.

She reached very slowly for Indy's hand and held it tight.

13: **Epilogue: Washington, D.C.**

Sun streamed through the windows of Colonel Musgrove's office. Outside, across a thick lawn, was a stand of cherry trees, and the morning sky was clear, a pale blue. Musgrove was seated behind his desk. Eaton had a chair to the side of the desk. There was another man, a man who stood leaning against the wall and who hadn't uttered a word; he had the sinister anonymity of a bureaucrat. He might have been rubber-stamped himself, Indy thought, *Powerful Civil Servant* in thick black letters on his brow.

"We appreciate your service," Musgrove said. "And the cash reimbursement—we assume it was satisfactory?"

Indy nodded and glanced first at Marion, then at Marcus Brody.

Brody said, "I don't understand yet why the museum can't have the Ark."

"It's someplace very safe," Eaton said evasively.

"That's a powerful force," Indy told him. "It has to be undersood. Analyzed. It isn't some game, you know."

Musgrove nodded. "We have our top men working on it right now."

"Name them," Indy said.

"For security reasons I can't."

"The Ark was slated for the museum. You agreed to that. Now you give us some crap about top men. Brody there—he's one of the best men in this whole field. Why doesn't he get a chance to work with your *top men*?"

"Indy," Brody said. "Leave it. Drop it."

"I won't," Indy said. "This whole affair cost me my favorite hat, for openers."

"I assure you, Jones, that the Ark is well protected. And its power—if we can accept your description of it—will be analyzed in due course."

"Due course," Indy said. "You remind me of letters I get from my lawyers."

"Look," Brody said, sounding strained, "all we want is the Ark for the museum. We want some reassurances, too, that no lasting damage will be done to it while in your possession—"

"You have them," Eaton said. "As for the Ark going to your museum, I'm afraid we will have to rethink our position."

A silence. A clock ticking. The faceless bureaucrat fiddled with his cuff links.

Indy said quietly, finally, "You don't know what you're sitting on, do you?"

He rose and helped Marion out of her chair.

"We'll be in touch, of course," Eaton said. "It was good of you to come. Your services are appreciated."

Outside in the warm sunlight, Marion took Indy's arm. Brody shuffled along beside them. Marion said, "Well, they aren't going to tell you anything, so maybe you should forget all about the Ark and get on with your life, Jones."

Indy glanced at Brody. He knew he had been tricked out of something that should have been his.

Brody said, "I guess they have their own good reasons for holding on to the Ark. It's a bitter disappointment, though."

Marion stopped, raised her leg and scratched her

heel a moment. She said to Indy, "Put your mind on something else for a change."

"Like what?"

"Like this," she said, and kissed him.

"It's not the Ark," he said and smiled. "But it'll have to do."

The wooden crate was stenciled on the side: TOP SECRET, ARMY INTELL, 9906753, DO NOT OPEN. It sat on a dolly, which the warehouseman pushed in front of him. He hardly paid any attention to the crate. His was a world filled with such crates, all of them meaninglessly stenciled. Numbers, numbers, secret codes. He had become more than immune to these hieroglyphics. He looked forward only to his weekly check. He was old, stooped, and very few things in life engrossed him. Certainly none of these crates did. There were hundreds of them filling the warehouse and he had no curiosity about any of them. Nobody did, it seemed. As far as he could tell nobody ever bothered to open any of them anyhow. They were stacked and left to pile up, rising from floor to ceiling. Crates and crates, hundreds and hundreds of the things. Gathering dust, getting cobwebbed. The man pushed his dolly and sighed. What difference did another crate make now? He found a space for it, slipped it in place, then he paused and stuck a finger in his ear, shaking the finger vigorously. Damn, he thought. He'd have to get his hearing checked.

He was convinced he'd heard a low humming noise.